White Lies

JULIE WETZEL

CHANGINGTIDES
PUBLISHING

White Lies

CHANGINGTIDES
PUBLISHING

ISBN: 978-1-63422-290-7
Cover Design: Marya Heidel
Interior Typography by: Courtney Knight
Editing by: Lauren Dootson

To Sherry.
You know why your name is here.
Love you!

One

How could I let my own flesh and blood do this to me? Molly pondered as she scanned over the menu. She dropped the thin booklet enough to watch the handsome man on the other side of the table worry the edge of his menu. His crystal blue eyes scanned across the page before rising to catch hers.

Phelix dropped his menu to the table. "Have you decided what you want, Mandy, darling?"

Molly let out a sigh. She still couldn't believe she'd let her twin sister talk her into this. How was she supposed to have dinner with her sister's boyfriend and not let him discover they'd switched places?

"I think so," Molly answered, closing her menu. She took a sip from her water glass, considering her choices. "The portabella stuffed ravioli with sun-dried tomatoes. What about you, Phelix?"

"Those are excellent," Phelix agreed. He

glanced down at the small print on his menu. "I think I'll have the lasagna if that's all right with you?" He raised his gaze and considered Molly with those gorgeous eyes.

Molly wanted to cry. *She* wanted the lasagna, but Mandy had spent most of the last few years as a vegan, so anything with meat was out of the question. The large mushrooms were the closest thing to flesh that her sister would consume, but she didn't mind others eating meat.

"Of course." Molly smiled biting back her frustration. Her sister was going to owe her big time for this.

"Would you like some wine to go with dinner?" Phelix asked, picking up the wine list.

"That would be lovely," Molly answered, leaving the choice of beverage up to her sister's boyfriend. She wasn't that much of a drinker, but her sister was. In fact, Mandy had met Phelix at a bar just over two months ago. She'd been so excited that she hadn't shut up about him since. Molly had finally put an end to her sister's ramblings when she started talking about how wonderful he was in bed. Those were some intimate details Molly felt she could live without. As it was, Molly hadn't been on a real date in years. She had dumped her last boyfriend when she found him banging one of the nurses in the medical center where they worked. That was the last time she was ever going to date a guy from her office. Molly hadn't found the heart to look for someone new yet.

"How about a nice Merlot?" Phelix offered.

Molly just barely kept the cringe off her face. Red wine went straight to her head, but Merlot was one of her sister's favorite wines. "Wonderful," she agreed, trying to make her faked smile reach her eyes.

"So how was work?" Molly asked, pushing her dinner date into small talk.

"Busy," Phelix said as he started off into the latest case at his law firm.

Molly listened to the rise and fall of his warm voice, wondering how her sister had ever landed such a hunk. Armed with their petite frames, long blonde hair, and gray eyes, she and her sister usually had the pick of any man they wanted, but Mandy had hit the jackpot with this one. Phelix was exactly what every girl wanted to bring home to mama. His chocolate hair was just long enough to hang into his face, and Molly could feel those crystal blue eyes burning into her soul. She could tell he worked out, even through his dark blue dress shirt and coat. After a few days without a shave, he could've passed for one of those *Chip 'n Dale* dancers Mandy had taken Molly to see for their birthday. The pause in his words drew Molly back from her fantasies of waving dollar bills as he stripped to some erotic beat.

Phelix looked at her expectantly.

Embarrassment colored Molly's cheeks when she couldn't pull the question he'd asked from her brain. "I'm sorry. Could you please repeat that?"

Amusement made Phelix's eyes twinkle, and he leaned back in his chair. "I asked how your day was."

"It was good," Molly said and started describing an average day pushing papers. Mandy and Molly were both medical coders who worked for the same company, but in two different offices. It wasn't a total lie, her day had been fine, but it was far from Mandy's day.

Mandy had come down with a stomach bug that kept her on the couch with a bucket by her head. Molly had tried to convince her to call Phelix and cancel their date, but Mandy refused, begging her sister to take her place for the evening.

Over the last few weeks, Phelix had broken several of his dates with Mandy. After the third time he'd begged off, Mandy threw a fit. She'd promptly informed him that if he broke another one, she would take it as being dumped and move on. Calling to cancel the evening after making such a fuss would be impossible. Only Mandy's tears and Molly's love for her sister landed Molly sitting in the upscale Italian restaurant in her twin's favorite red dress and impossibly high heels.

"That sounds interesting," Phelix encouraged Molly to continue.

Taking her cues from Phelix, she launched into a story about the girls in Mandy's office. Mandy liked to chatter about everything and Molly tried to imitate her sister as best she could. It usually wasn't hard to fool people when they swapped places. Their voices were nearly identical, and they had spent almost every day of their life together. This wasn't the first time Molly had taken her sister's place at a social function. It was, however, the first time that social function was with someone her sister was sleeping with. Molly had pointed this out, but her sister had an answer for that.

Although they had spent a lot of time on the phone, Mandy and Phelix had only seen each other a handful of occasions during the few months they had been going out. Phelix's job had been keeping him extremely busy. Most of their dates had been either in dimly lit bars or the darkness of Phelix's bedroom. They hadn't been out to a nice sit-down dinner yet, so this was the perfect time for Molly to fill in. All she had to do was eat with him, pretend to be Mandy, and make sure to go home alone at the end of the evening. Mandy had even given Molly permission to kiss him good night.

The arrival of the waiter gave Molly a good reason to stop talking. She'd never been so glad to see a plate of food. At least now she could busy her mouth with eating and not carrying on aimlessly like her sister usually did.

"Thank you for having dinner with me tonight," Phelix said as he cut into his lasagna. "I'm sorry I've had to break so many of our dates recently."

Molly nodded around the bite of ravioli she had just stuck in her mouth.

"Work has been so busy. There's a critical case coming up, and I've been working overtime trying to get it together."

"Thank you for asking," Molly answered as soon as her mouth was clear. "I understand how important work can be."

Phelix raised an eyebrow and gave her a questioning look. "I thought you were upset about me breaking so many of our dates."

Molly refrained from the face-palm she felt she deserved. She'd forgotten that was what had gotten her into this mess. "Of course I don't like being put aside for a job," Molly retorted, trying to cover her error, "but that doesn't mean that I don't understand the need for it every once in a while." She stirred the sauce on her plate before meeting his gaze again. "Just try not to do it too often." She put a sharp edge of warning in her eyes, but had a hard time keeping it when a smile broke out across Phelix's face.

He picked up his wine glass and held it out. "Of course not."

Molly raised her glass and met his gaze with a warm smile before joining him in the toast. Setting the glass back on the table, she returned to her meal with the hopes of making it the rest of the way through dinner in a manner in which her sister would approve.

"THANK YOU FOR A WONDERFUL DINNER," MOLLY SAID AS Phelix opened the car door. "I had a really great time."

Phelix offered his hand to help her from the car. "You're quite welcome."

Molly took it and let him lift her to her feet. She hated the skyscraper heels her sister had paired with the short, red dress.

Wrapping his arms around her, Phelix held Molly tightly. "I had a wonderful time too."

This was part of the date she'd been dreading

all night. It hadn't taken much for Molly to realize that his touch made her skin tingle in dangerous ways. Being wrapped in his arms brought her much too close to that delicious body her sister had gone on about. Just the feel of him surrounding her sent her mind off to places it shouldn't go.

Her body tightened as his warm breath brushed against her skin. A zing of electricity tingled along her nerves as his warm lips captured hers.

His passion-filled kiss weakened her knees, and she was glad he held her so tightly. She wasn't sure her legs would hold without his support. By the time he finished, she was clinging to him, breathless with need.

"Are you sure I can't keep you company tonight?" Phelix asked as he placed another light kiss on the corner of Molly's mouth.

Desire swirled through Molly as she weighed her options. Following the call of the warmth pulling deep inside would be easy. She longed to take this man upstairs and let him do all of those things her sister had described, but the pain it would cause her sister made her force the desire away. "I'm sure," Molly said as she pulled herself together. She pushed against his solid chest, making him loosen his hold. "Unfortunately, I have to head to the office early tomorrow for some make-up work," she explained, giving the excuse her sister had decided on.

"I understand," Phelix said. He laid another soft kiss on her lips before letting her go. "I'll call you tomorrow."

A twinge of regret darkened her mood as she slipped from his hold.

His fingers lingered on her arm as she went and his smile held a hint of disappointment. "Have a good night."

A longing sigh slipped out as Molly stepped away from his touch. "Good night, Phelix," she said as she turned toward her apartment complex. Thankfully, she and her sister lived in the same building. As she moved, the tip of her stiletto heel caught in the soft caulking in the sidewalk. Unable to compensate for the uneven footing, Molly's ankle gave out, and she squeaked as she crashed to the ground.

"Mandy!" Phelix cried as he rushed to her aid.

She felt his hand flip the hem of her skirt down over her hip and thigh. A blush the same shade as her dress rushed over Molly's face.

"Are you all right?" Phelix asked as he knelt by her side.

Pushing up from the ground, Molly drew her legs beneath her. "Yeah," she said, turning her hands over to look at her palms. Scuff marks graced the heels of her hands where she'd tried to catch herself. They were angry and red, but not actively bleeding. "I think so." She turned her attention to the towering heels that caused her fall. The stupid shoes were in one piece, but her ankle hurt badly.

Phelix took one of her injured hands and turned it toward the light from the building.

"I'm okay," Molly said, pulling it from his grasp. She rubbed her palms together, dislodging the grit embedded in her skin.

Gathering up her fallen clutch, Phelix stood and held his hand out to Molly. "Let me help you."

Pausing to think, she stared at his hand before taking the offered assistance. The scrapes on her hands didn't bother her, but she was worried about the pain in her ankle. Molly gasped as her injured leg throbbed under her weight. She teetered off balance when the ankle couldn't take the load.

Phelix caught her before she could fall again.

"I think I hurt my ankle," Molly admitted as she grabbed him. She glared down at the stubborn body part refusing to work properly.

Phelix let out an amused snort. "Let's get you inside." He handed her the purse and shot her a mischievous grin before scooping her off her feet. "So where are we going?" he asked, mounting the steps to the entranceway.

Molly clenched her jaw in fear. She worried about giving him directions to her apartment, but she couldn't see a way around it. There was no way she could make it up the three flights of steps on her own. Relaxing in his arms, she directed him to her apartment. Her sister held the unit one floor down, so hopefully, if Phelix ever came back, he wouldn't notice the slight change in location. "You really don't have to do this," Molly muttered, as he carried her up the steps.

Phelix squeezed her as he reached her landing. "I couldn't just leave you lying on the street," he teased.

"That's not what I meant," Molly said in a huff. "You didn't have to carry me. I could've made it with some help." There was a chance the ankle would hold her if she got rid of those heels.

"It's best not to stress it," Phelix said. The teasing tone had vanished from his voice. He smiled gently. "Besides, this is nice," he said, cuddling her again.

Molly drew in a ragged breath. "Thank you," she said trying to get a grip on her physical reaction. Even injured, he had a profound effect on her. Clearing her throat, she fished in her clutch for her keys.

Phelix shifted her in his arms and snagged the keys from her fingers.

"Hey!" she cried out in surprise.

Ignoring her protests, Phelix worked the key into the lock and pushed the door open with his shoulder.

Letting out a resigned breath, Molly just held on as her sister's boyfriend carried her into the darkened apartment. "I could've done that," she complained, squirming in Phelix's arms as the door shut behind them and cast them into near darkness.

He shifted her in his arms again and let her feet drop to the floor but didn't release her completely. "You shouldn't be standing on that ankle," Phelix insisted. Thin light streamed in through the curtains making the room manageable as Molly limped her way through the modestly furnished apartment to her couch and matching loveseat. A wooden coffee table sat on the floor between the couch and an entertainment center. Two matching end tables held old fashion crystal lamps on either end of the sofa. Phelix pushed the coffee table out of the way as he helped Molly to the couch.

Reaching over, Molly clicked on the lamp. "Oh hell," she said as the soft light reflected on a line of dark blood trailing from a tear in her silk stocking. She'd been sure the twisted ankle and scraped palms were her only injuries.

Kneeling down, Phelix pulled his handkerchief from his pocket, placed it over the bleeding wound, and pressed down hard to stop the blood. "Hold this," he said, moving his hand so Molly could take the cloth. Once both hands were free, Phelix reached for her swollen ankle. Slipping off the impossibly high heel, he carefully pressed his long fingers into the joint.

Molly hissed in pain when he found a particularly tender spot.

"Does this hurt?" Phelix asked as he gripped Molly's foot and moved it around gently.

"Yes!" Molly gasped when he bent it inward.

Phelix prodded the sore skin. "It looks like you might have sprained it." He rubbed her foot soothingly before standing up from the floor. "Do you have a first aid kit?" he asked, glancing around the room.

Molly pointed toward the darkened hallway. "There's a box of first aid stuff in the bottom of the closet."

Pulling off his jacket, Phelix laid it over the back of the loveseat and went to find bandages.

Lifting the handkerchief from her knee, Molly looked at the cut. It wasn't as bad as she'd first thought. She pulled at her stockings trying to separate the shredded silk from the gash.

"Peroxide?" Phelix called from the hallway.

"There's a bottle in the bathroom under the sink," Molly yelled back. Giving up on cleaning the wound, she laid the handkerchief back over the cut. She was going to have to take the stockings off before she could do much good.

It didn't take long for Phelix to come back with a bottle of peroxide and the box of supplies Molly had squirreled away. "Why don't you have a proper first aid kit?" he asked, dropping the collection on the table.

Molly shrugged. "Never needed one." Her heart fluttered as he pulled off his tie and rolled up his sleeves. She did her best to stamp down on her feelings, but it didn't do her much good.

Phelix knelt on the floor to look at her leg. "You shouldn't wait until you need a first aid kit to get one," he said as he took the cloth from Molly's hand. "It's something every home needs."

Hanging her head, Molly nodded. "I'm sorry," she muttered.

"It's all right," Phelix replied in a gentler tone. "I'll get you a first aid kit," he promised as he laid his bloody handkerchief on the table.

Molly shivered as Phelix caressed her thigh just above her injured knee.

"Let's see what we can do about this."

"Hey!" Molly cried out when Phelix slipped his hand under her skirt. She squirmed, trying to get away from his intruding hand.

His hands gripped her leg, preventing her from pushing off with her injured foot. "Be still," Phelix warned with a pointed look. When she'd stopped moving, he slipped his hand back up her skirt and popped the clasp holding her thigh high stocking in place.

Molly relaxed when she realized what he was doing. She held still as he worked the second clasp loose. "I'm sorry," she said, feeling foolish. Of course, he needed to get the stocking off before he could bandage the cut. "I guess I've had a little too much wine."

Phelix patted her leg gently. "It's all right," he soothed as he slipped his other hand between her thighs to the top of her stockings. "Although, I do like the fact you wear thigh highs. I can think of some interesting things we could do with these on." He shot her a devilish grin as his knuckles rubbed against the lace covering her most sensitive parts.

Molly sucked in a sharp breath at the unexpected touch. Anticipation and dread tore at her. She let the air out as his fingers pulled back and slid under the band of her stocking.

"Maybe next time," he said, pulling the silk down her thigh. Very carefully, he lifted the soft material over the cut and slipped the stocking free of Molly's leg.

Trying to clear her mind of the suggestive thoughts he'd spawned, Molly looked at the angry red mark on her knee. The sight of the laceration cooled some of the desire burning in her. "I did a number on it."

"That's not so bad," Phelix said as he touched the injury. "It just needs cleaning up." Retrieving a washcloth from the pile on the table, he dabbed the wound with the warm, wet fabric.

Biting her lip, Molly whimpered, trying not to cry out in pain.

Phelix looked up at her. "It will be okay," he promised. Pushing up from the floor, he caught her lips in a reassuring kiss.

Leaning forward, Molly accepted the offered comfort. Another pang of desire hit as Phelix settled back to the floor to finish tending her wound. She really shouldn't be having these feelings toward her sister's boyfriend, but she couldn't help herself. It was impossible to ignore the way his fingers brushed over her uninjured skin as he worked. Every touch sent tingles of pleasure racing through her veins. "Thank you," she said as Phelix cleaned and disinfected the cut.

"You're welcome," Phelix said as he found a bandage large enough to cover the injured area. He glanced at the discarded shoe responsible for

Molly's fall. "You really should be more careful in those things."

She sighed heavily. "I know." She glanced at the heels with hatred. "I'm not used to wearing them. But my sis—" Suddenly realizing her error, Molly bit off her words before she spilled the beans. Mandy was fond of her shoes and almost always wore high heels.

Phelix glanced up at the unnatural break in her speech.

"I mean," she quickly backtracked to cover her slip, "I'm not used to these shoes. I just got them to match this dress." Molly shifted on the couch showing off the red dress as much as she could without getting up.

Amusement lit Phelix's eyes, and he moved closer. "And you look absolutely amazing in it." Leaning forward, he planted another powerful kiss on Molly's mouth.

She shivered as the passion in his kiss resonated inside her, urging her on. Molly's world was spinning by the time he broke the kiss. Closing her eyes, she leaned back into the cushions to recover.

Phelix caressed her cheek before sitting back on the floor to finish bandaging her foot.

Drawing in a deep breath, Molly forced her eyes open and watched as Phelix rummaged through her box of medical stuff. She needed to get a grip on herself before things got out of control.

Phelix pulled out a roll of wide tape. "This should work."

"For what?" Molly asked as he tore off several long lengths and stuck them to the edge of the table. Her sister had bought that tape to help with some strappy Halloween costumes they'd worn. The tops had been too skimpy to wear a bra, and that tape had been just the support they'd needed.

"To tape up your ankle." Lifting Molly's foot, Phelix laid several strips of the tape down the outside of her ankle.

Molly watched in fascination as he wrapped the tape around her foot and leg. "Is that what it's for?"

Phelix laughed. "Of course." He shot her a cheeky grin. "What did you think sports tape was for?"

She shrugged, unwilling to tell Phelix how she'd used it. "Where did you learn to do that?" Molly asked in an attempt to distract him from his question.

This time Phelix shrugged. "It's a skill everyone needs to know," he explained. "This is basic first aid."

Molly nodded. "Maybe you can teach me

sometime?" she suggested. She liked the idea of getting to know Phelix better. The reality of her situation hit, and she sighed. Even if he agreed, she wouldn't get that lesson. Her sister was actually serious about this man, and she probably wouldn't see him again after he was done bandaging her up.

"I would enjoy that," Phelix said. He sat back and looked at her leg. "All done."

Molly inspected his handy work. The tape crisscrossed back and forth over her foot, holding it in place. She tried to move her ankle but found that it was bound pretty tight. Molly shifted forward on the couch, ready to get up.

Placing a hand on her hip, Phelix pushed her back into the cushions. "Not yet," he warned. He gave her a demanding look. "Hands."

Molly cocked her head and turned her hands over to look at the abrasions on her palms. They really weren't that bad. "They're fine," she said, rubbing them together.

"It doesn't matter," Phelix insisted. "They need to be cleaned." He held his hand out for hers.

With a suffering sigh that made him smile, she gave in to his demands.

Phelix took his time cleaning and bandaging Molly's palms.

Shaking her head, Molly watched as he taped

thick pads over her wounds. His efforts would last for about five minutes while she saw him out. After that, she would have to pull the bandages off to get ready for bed. The tape and gauze wouldn't last through the frigid shower she needed to quiet the longing Phelix's attention had caused. "Are we done now?" Molly asked. She watched as Phelix gathered her medical supplies and placed them back in the box.

Phelix snickered. "Yes." He stood up and held out his hands.

Molly kicked off the other heel and let him help her from the couch. Now all she had to do was see him out, and they could call it a night. "Thank you," she said as she stood up. Squeaking loudly, she clutched at Phelix as he swept her legs out from under her again. Rattled by the motion, it took Molly a moment to realize that Phelix hadn't just picked her up; he was carrying her toward the hallway. "Um..." she said as they moved farther into the apartment.

"You should stay off that ankle for the evening," Phelix insisted. Placing his shoulder on the door, he pushed his way into her bedroom.

Any protests Molly could have made froze on her lips as Phelix spun around and sat down on the edge of her bed. She gasped when he brought her down on his lap, so he was staring straight into her eyes. The fact that he was her sister's boyfriend nearly had her flipping out of his lap, but that same panic stopped her. She stared at him with wide eyes as her mind spun. What was she going to do now? On the one hand, this was leading to the very compromising situation she was trying to avoid, but on the other, she had to think like her sister to keep their lie from being discovered. Unable to come up with an answer, she held her breath to see what would happen.

"You look absolutely amazing," Phelix whispered.

She could feel the desire in his voice as he caressed her cheek.

Slipping his fingers in the hair at the back of her neck, he pulled her to him for a soul-shattering kiss.

The heat from his skin burned along her jaw as the passion from his kiss addled her mind. Her dilemma vanished. She knew she should stop him, but she just couldn't bring herself to do it. The last little bit of her mind that was working properly clamored at her. Things had just gone too far to stop. If she pushed him away now, she would only cause issues for her sister later. Refusing him wasn't something Mandy would do, even if she was slightly injured. This was happening, and Molly would have to explain it to her sister tomorrow and hope Mandy forgave her.

The real trouble was Molly's own feelings. She didn't want him to stop. Phelix made her feel things that she hadn't experienced in a long time. Giving in to his demanding lips and her building desires, Molly melted into his embrace. There would be trouble for her actions later, but, at the moment, she didn't care.

Molly reveled in their shared desire as the intensity of their kiss increased.

Twisting, Phelix leaned her back to the bed. His hand ran down her back caressing her through the material of her dress. He nibbled at her lip before pulling back and gazing at her.

Molly swallowed hard as she met his desire-darkened eyes. She relaxed back into the bedding as he pushed them into a more comfortable position.

"So beautiful," Phelix whispered. His free hand slipped up her side and trailed across her chest before moving to caress the hair back from her face.

Molly let out a sigh as he leaned over and rekindled their kiss. Her hands caught his sides, and she rubbed him through his dress shirt. His lips twitched against hers, and he pulled away from her mouth to nibble his way across her cheek and down over her jaw.

Swallowing hard, Molly tried to remember how to breathe without moaning. The feelings boiling through her were unlike anything she could recall. She didn't have much time to think. His teeth grazed the sensitive skin of her throat, drawing out another gasp. She rolled her head, and gave him more access. She could feel his lip curve into a smile as his fingers slipped under the straps of her dress. Her eyes fluttered shut as the sensations assaulted her senses.

Molly gasped as Phelix's mouth moved down her neck to her collar bone. Her eyes sprang open, and she tensed up when the material of her dress shifted out of the way without resistance. When had he unzipped the back of her dress?

Phelix hushed her as he pulled the red material down, exposing the black lace of her bra. Molly relaxed, glad that her sister had insisted on the sensual item. She would have been happy with something more sensible, but the pleased noise Phelix let out made Molly happy that she had given into her sister's fashion demands. The tips of his fingers rubbed across the soft flesh of her chest, making her moan.

Running her hands up around Phelix's shoulders, she curled her fingers into the fine hair at the back of his neck.

Phelix pulled the dress farther down Molly's

body.

Slipping her arms free of the shoulder straps, she let him slide her out of the dress before tangling her fingers back in his hair.

Pressing a hot kiss into the curve at the top of her breast, Phelix tugged on her left cup pulling the material back so his lips could find the swollen tip of her nipple.

The scrape of his teeth made Molly gasp, and she curled her fingers deeper into his hair and held him in place. Her blood raced through her veins and drove her on.

Sucking hard on her nipple, Phelix let it pop from his mouth before cupping her freed breast in his hand and kneading the tender flesh.

She drew in a measured breath as his thumb and index came together around her nipple and pinched it with just enough pressure to send electricity shooting through her body. As he toyed with one breast, he shifted his attention to the other, still trapped inside the black lace bra. A gentle tug had that mound free and in his mouth.

Molly moaned again as he drove shivers of pleasure to places deep inside her. Pushed by her desires, she tilted her hips up and pressed them into him.

Phelix groaned as her hips made contact with his body. The hand that had been caressing her breast trailed down her stomach to her waist. He gripped her hip hard and pulled it up, so she pressed into him again.

Another sound of pleasure escaped from Molly's lips. Warmth had formed deep in her core, and she could feel the wetness seeping out, preparing her for what was coming.

Phelix's stimulating attention shifted again as he slid down the length of her body. His lips worshiped every inch of her body as he worked his way down the smooth expanse of Molly's stomach. Pausing for a moment, he slipped his tongue into her navel and tugged her dress down over her hips.

Color flashed behind Molly's eyes as an unpleasant sensation raced up from her hip. The contrast of pain and pleasure made her tense up and she hissed in discomfort.

Phelix froze above her. Worry colored his eyes as he met hers.

"Hip," Molly explained as she relaxed.

Moving back, he slid her dress off and ran his hand over her hip, feeling the area where she'd met the pavement.

She cringed when he touched the purpling skin. It was uncomfortable but didn't really hurt.

Pulling his hand back, he placed a kiss over the slight wound. "It'll be okay," he reassured her.

Molly cracked a grin and raised an eyebrow. "Oh, so you're a doctor now?" she teased.

Phelix grinned mischievously. "Yes," he purred, "now hold still so I can give you something for that pain." Sliding the rest of the way off the bed, he wrapped his arms around her thighs and gently pulled her to the edge of the bed.

She giggled as he pressed his face up between her legs. Wiggling back, she tried to get away as he mouthed her playfully through her lace panties, but he held her in place. Her laughter turned to passionate moans as he found his way around the material and into the wet warmth waiting below.

Once she stopped fighting, Phelix relaxed his hold on her legs and peeled the remaining stocking from Molly's leg before going back for the scrap of lace blocking him.

Molly's hips rocked up as he relieved her of that last remaining cloth. The night air licking at her delicate parts were quickly replaced with Phelix's warm breath as he appreciated the treasures he'd found.

"So lucky," Phelix whispered. The words tickled across her exposed skin before he ran his hot tongue up between her folds.

Molly gasped at the changing sensations. Her whole body twitched as he licked her tender flesh.

Slipping his hands up under her hips, Phelix

rolled them up so he could have better access to her core.

Unable to reach him without sitting up, Molly balled her fists into the blanket and held on as he explored all of her body with his tongue. Just when she thought she could take no more of his nimble mouth, one of his fingers found the opening at her center. Shutting her eyes, she gasped as the digit wormed its way inside her. Molly moaned and bent so she could tangle her hand into his brown hair as he carefully pumped his finger in and out.

Looking down at the man pressed between her thighs, she caught the light from the other room reflecting in his crystal eyes. Embarrassment stole over her as she realized that he was watching her. Every moan, every twitch, every weird face she made, he was taking it all in.

The moment of embarrassment didn't last long as he slipped a second finger inside her to dance with the first. Her world only lasted a few seconds longer as the orgasm ripped through her, making her body convulse around his wiggling digits.

Moving back, Phelix stroked the last of the spasms from Molly's body before sliding his fingers from her.

Through half-lidded eyes, Molly watched as he stood up and sucked his fingers clean. She shivered at the sight and closed her eyes, waiting for her world to come together again.

When his weight pressed down on the bed, she opened her eyes and found that he'd stripped out of his clothing. The light shining down the hallway reflected off the sculptured muscles of his chest and stomach as he moved above her. Her eyes flashed down his body, and a pang of panic cut through her aroused state. She had been with men before, but it had been a while, and none of them were anywhere near the size of Phelix. "Be gentle," she pleaded.

"Always," he whispered before pressing his lips to hers.

The tang of her own juices filled her mouth, and she licked her lips as Phelix wrapped his arm around her back and drew her up the bed. Molly grabbed his shoulders as he maneuvered them to the pillows. Once there, she wiggled until she was comfortable again. The band of her bra cut into her over-sensitive skin, irritating her. Growling in frustration, Molly twisted so she could get her hand near the strap and release the band.

Phelix groaned when the clasp popped open. "Nice," he whispered, pulling the black material away from her skin and chucking it across the room. Pressing to her lips, he claimed them again as he lowered his body against Molly's.

She could feel his hardened state pressing into

her belly as he moved. Raising her knees, she gave him the space he needed.

Lifting himself up, he moved to his knees. He groaned hungrily into her mouth as the tip of his member caressed the soft skin of her stomach. Pulling back the hand he'd tangled in her hair, he ran it down her body. He paused long enough to flick the tip of her nipple before continuing down between her legs. Rubbing her again, he grasped his hardened length and guided the tip to her opening.

Molly gasped as he pushed into her. He felt much bigger than he looked as her delicate flesh gave way to his intrusion.

"So tight," Phelix moaned as he pressed more of his length into her.

Molly was glad that he took it slow and gave her body time to adjust to his unusual size. She was sure that he was going to split her in half, but he somehow managed to get most of the way in before pausing. One final thrust seated him completely inside her. She cried out when he hit bottom, but he didn't give her time to focus on the pain as he started to move.

At first, his strokes were short and slow, but they quickly found a solid rhythm as Molly's body adjusted to him.

Scrambling for something to hold on to, her

hands found purchase on his solid back as another orgasm sent her over the edge.

Slowing, Phelix lingered in his movements as she quivered around him. When most of the delicious spasms had passed, he picked the tempo up again pushing her over that wall once more. He hissed as her nails raked over his skin in her passion. This time he didn't give her time to recover. Crushing his lips to hers, he picked up the pace until Molly's world shattered and left her screaming into the night.

She clenched her legs around Phelix as he reached his peak. Warmth exploded deep inside her and they hung on the edge of oblivion together before collapsing into a heap on the bed.

Molly's mind was numb as she came down from her high. Her trembling limbs wouldn't listen and she could still feel Phelix deep inside her, but she was at peace with that for the moment. As feeling returned to her extremities, her fingers softened against his back, and she held him gently. A hint of regret colored her euphoria, but she pushed it away. She would have plenty of time to dwell on her transgressions later.

Sighing contently, Phelix rolled, so he was no longer resting on top of her.

Molly shivered as his length slipped from her body, leaving her empty inside. That feeling rose to her chest, and she drew in a breath to keep it from overtaking her. She'd never had this type of passion with anyone else, and the realization that it was with a man she could never have hit her hard. She closed her eyes to keep the tears from spilling out. She bit her lip as Phelix rolled to his back and drew her in against him.

She cuddled with him, recovering from their mixed passion. His warmth was both enjoyable and agonizing. Throughout the evening she had grown to like him, but she knew that he would leave soon and that made her sad. Although they shouldn't have spent the evening together, she discovered she didn't want it to end. A ping of jealousy swept through her. Her sister was one lucky woman. There weren't a lot of men who were both kind and good in bed. Feelings of anger and remorse warred inside her, but Molly let them out in a long breath. She'd have time tomorrow to talk with her sister about this whole situation. She shivered as the cooler air of the room lapped the sweat from her body.

Phelix grabbed the edge of the comforter they were laying on and dragged the loose end over them.

Molly sighed again as the material blocked out the draft and she gave in to sleep, cuddled in against Phelix's warm side.

"I SLEPT WITH YOUR BOYFRIEND," MOLLY ADMITTED.

Red colored Mandy's vision as she stopped and stared at her sister. Molly was stretched out on the couch in comfy looking sweats, gorging herself on a pint of Phish Food ice cream. Coming over, Mandy sat on the sofa next to her sister. "What happened?" she asked with a sigh. Kicking off her heels, she picked up a throw pillow and cuddled it in her lap.

"I tried to send him off with just a kiss," Molly explained as she stared down into the mostly empty pint of ice cream, "and it almost worked. Until I fell." Lifting her foot, she rested it on the edge of the couch.

Worry cooled Mandy's anger as she stared down at the medical tape wrapped around her sister's leg. "What happened?" she asked as she reached out to touch Molly's wound. She knew her sister could be clumsy, but didn't see how she could've hurt herself during a simple dinner.

"I caught one of your heels in the sidewalk," Molly grumbled. She stabbed her spoon into the melting dessert. "Phelix carried me home and bandaged me up."

"He's so sweet," Mandy gushed. Her heart

melted at the thought of him tending her sister's injury, but Molly's words echoed in her head. She squeezed the pillow tighter and waited for her sister to continue.

"He's sweet all right," Molly agreed as she scraped together another bite of ice cream. "He carried me upstairs, bandaged my foot, and took me straight to bed so I wouldn't hurt myself more." Molly stuck the dark chocolate fish in her mouth and sucked on it hard.

Mandy could hear the bitter note in her sister's words. She held her tongue until Molly let out the comment she had brewing.

"How was I supposed to get out of that one?" Molly finally snapped.

Mandy drew in a deep breath and let it out. She hung her head and thought about how to respond. She was furious, but she didn't dare take that anger out on Molly. It was *her* fault that her twin was in a situation where sex with her man was a possibility. She'd hoped that Molly could have avoided that outcome. She knew her sister wouldn't have had sex with Phelix if she could have figured a way out of it that didn't expose their switch.

"Point," Mandy finally conceded. She wanted to be mad, but she also understood how Molly ended up in bed with Phelix. Phelix could be a very demanding individual, and if he had pushed, Molly would have done what she felt her twin would do—give in like a wet paper bag. Taking in another deep breath, she forced herself to accept the situation without taking it out on Mandy. They had, after all, shared almost everything in their life. She could live with sharing her boyfriend with her twin as long as it only happened once. "So how was it?" Mandy asked, looking up at her sister.

Molly's eyes nearly popped out of her head. "How was what?"

A little bit of sadistic joy filled Mandy as she pressed her sister for information. "The sex," she clarified. "How was it?" She wasn't happy about the whole affair, but making her sister squirm eased some of the anger in her heart.

Molly blushed and stared down into the paper container. She dug out another frozen fish and refused to meet Mandy's eyes. "It was good."

Mandy swatted her sister's leg urging her into telling the truth. "Come on!" She shot her sister a knowing smile and wiggled her eyebrows at her.

Molly squirmed on the couch but finally gave in. "All right!" she huffed. "It was the best sex I've had in years!"

Mandy giggled as she crossed her legs and turned to face her sister. "It's the only sex you've had in years." Molly didn't rise to the verbal jab, but Mandy didn't expect her to. Instead, her sister came back with something that made Mandy grin.

"Damn it, Mandy. That man can do things with his tongue that should be outlawed."

The blush on Molly's face went clear to her ears. Mandy squeezed her pillow as she recalled some of the more interesting things Phelix had done with his tongue. "I know," she said. Leaning forward, she pinned her with her eyes. "So tell me everything."

"No," Molly said indignantly. The color on her face deepened.

Upset that her sister wouldn't share, Mandy released the pillow and smacked it into her lap. "Come on," she whined.

A pained look crossed Molly's face. "I don't want to go there."

"But what if Phelix asks?" Mandy pushed.

Molly let out a long sigh and caved to her twin's demand. "All I'm going to say is the man knows how to knock a woman for a loop."

Mandy gasped. "You passed out!" Phelix had brought her to the very edge of oblivion on several occasions, but hadn't managed to knock her out. The glare Molly shot her could have burnt flesh.

"No," Molly huffed, "but it came very close."

She jabbed her spoon in her ice cream as she gave up the details Mandy wanted. "It was some of the best sex I've ever had. I couldn't move for a while afterward, and I don't remember when he left."

A sliver of ice stabbed Mandy in the heart, and she sat up. "You mean he stayed the night?" She and Phelix had been having a fair amount of sex, but the evenings always ended with her going home. She hadn't had the pleasure of waking up next to him yet.

Molly gave her sister a pained look. "I have no idea," she admitted. "I vaguely remember him pulling the covers over us before falling asleep. When I woke up this morning, he was gone."

The shard of dread melted in a sigh of relief. Her sister hadn't experienced something Mandy hadn't.

"But, he really is a sweetheart though," Molly continued. "Not only did he set my alarm so I wouldn't oversleep, he left a glass of water sitting on the table with some painkillers for my leg and a note."

"A note?" Mandy asked. She was super curious to see what he had to say. She'd never gotten a note or letter from Phelix before.

"It's in the bedroom," Molly nodded her head toward the hallway. "It basically said that he had a great night and told me to take it easy on my ankle for a while." She looked down at Mandy's discarded heels. "You might want to go with flats for the next day or so."

Mandy followed her sister's gaze down to her shoes. She almost always wore heels, but she did have a couple of cute ballet flats that were super comfy. She made a mental note to dig them out for the next few days. "So what else?" she asked as she looked back up at her sister. She was dying to know everything that had happened during the date.

Molly laughed. "Not very much," she admitted. "We chatted about work and ate. Overall, it was a very pleasant evening." A tortured smile turned up the corner of Molly's mouth. "Even with the unexpected bout of sex."

A horrible thought passed through Mandy's mind, and she shoved the pillow behind her back. "Get dressed," she said as she got up from the couch and retrieved her shoes. "You can tell me everything on the way." Shoving her feet in her heels, she got up and turned to take the carton of ice cream from her sister's hand.

Alarm crinkled Molly's face. "To where?" she asked as she started to move.

"The drugstore," Mandy answered. She placed the melting ice cream on the table and pulled her sister into motion.

"Why?" Molly asked as Mandy pushed her down the hall to the bedroom.

"If I know Phelix, he didn't use any protection," Mandy explained. She and Phelix had had the whole STD and pregnancy discussion early on. Mandy had made sure to get on a good birth control, but she knew her sister wasn't taking any at the moment.

Tension tightened Molly's shoulders. "Oh God, Mandy!" she gasped. "What am I going to do?"

Mandy patted her on the back, but didn't stop pushing her along. "It's all right," she soothed her sister. "You have some time to get a 'Plan B' pill, but they work best if you take them right away."

Molly relaxed and hurried into the bedroom. "What would I do without you?"

"You wouldn't be having sex on the first date," Mandy teased.

"Yeah, about that, let's not do this again." Molly shook her head. "I like your boyfriend, but I don't think I can handle another night like that."

"Good point," Mandy agreed. "I think I'd have to get mad at you for sleeping with my boyfriend a second time."

"Hey!" Molly yelled. She tossed her sweatshirt at her sister.

Laughing again, Mandy dodged away from the

frumpy shirt and watched as her sister found more suitable clothing. Now all they had to do was get Molly her emergency contraceptives, and they could put this whole messy business behind them.

two

A FAMILIAR MALE VOICE CARRIED A NAME ACROSS THE LOBBY making Molly freeze. Shock tightened her shoulders as she turned away from her coworkers to see who was calling her sister's name. She couldn't believe her eyes when she saw the tall brunet heading her way.

"What do we have here?" one of her coworkers teased as the handsome man closed on them.

"Nothing," Molly hissed, trying to discourage her friends from saying anything to give her away. Stepping away from her friends, she went to greet the last person she expected to see during lunch.

"Phelix," she called in greeting, "what are you doing here?" She tried to keep her tone to enjoyment and surprise. It had only been two days since their evening together, and she didn't know how to handle this surprise meeting. This was not the Monday she was hoping for.

He took a quick glance around the lobby of the

medical center before answering her. "I'm here to see one of the doctors," Phelix said as he met Molly's eyes again. "He's an old friend." Reaching out, he slid his hand down Molly's arm and took her hand. "What are you doing here?" His eyes slid down her body to where her ankle peaked out from under her long, flowered skirt. "Is your ankle still bothering you?"

Molly shook her head. "No. But I did get an ankle brace to help." She slid her foot forward, showing off the support device sticking out of the top of her flat soled shoes. She was painfully aware of her outfit as his gaze moved over her. Her fitted top and long skirt were perfect for her work setting. They were both comfortable and professional, but they weren't anything like her sister's trendy style. Thankfully, Phelix didn't seem to notice.

"That's good," he said. He turned puzzled eyes to her again "So what are you doing here?"

Licking her lower lip, Molly paused, trying to come up with a good excuse for her sister to be here. Although they both worked for the same medical chain, Mandy's office was across town. The sounds of her friends giggling behind her didn't help her ability to think. "I'm going to lunch," Molly said, trying to distract him from the question. A soft pat on her shoulder drew her attention away from Phelix. She turned to see her coworker shooting her a knowing grin.

"We'll catch you later."

Before Molly could say anything, her friends turned and abandoned her to Phelix's company. She opened her mouth to yell at them, but she paused before anything came out. Her friends were probably trying to help her hook up with a handsome man for lunch, but they didn't realize the mistake he'd made. Her only means of escape was walking away, but she didn't dare call them back. She turned to look at Phelix, but he was still watching her friends walk away. She had just a moment to decide what to do.

He'd called her by her sister's name. That mean he still thought she was her twin and there was overwhelming evidence to prove she was the woman he'd gone out with this past weekend. If she corrected him now, he would know about the lie she'd told. And that could destroy her sister's relationship. If she had any hopes of saving things, she was going to have to lie again.

"It looks like you're on your own now," Phelix said he turned back to Molly. "Would you care to join me for lunch?" He shot her an encouraging smile.

Molly drew in a slow breath and forced a smile to her face. "I would love that," she said.

She would play the part of her twin one more time, but her sister was going to owe her big time for this.

Phelix's eyes lit up with joy. "Excellent." Leaning in, he placed a light kiss on her cheek. "I know of a nice place just down the street." Pulling her to his side, he wrapped her hand around his arm and started out of the building. Once they were on the street, he gave her a sideways glance and asked again. "So what are you doing here?"

Molly rubbed her fingers over the gray material of his suit coat as she thought. There was no way she was going to sidetrack him from his question, so she tried to think of a good reason Mandy would be there. After a few steps, an idea hit her. "I'm filling in," she said, spinning up a plausible story. "One of the girls in our sister office is out on medical leave, so I was sent over to help take up the slack." It wasn't completely untrue. One of the girls in her office was out on leave after a bad car wreck, and someone had been sent from Mandy's office to help with the extra workload. She held her breath and walked on in silence, waiting to see if Phelix would buy her story

He turned his head and gave her a warm smile. "That's very sweet of you."

Molly let out the breath. It looked like she'd gotten away with another lie. Now she just had to remember to inform her sister. "Thank you," she said, "but it's not a matter of being nice. When the boss says jump, I jump."

Phelix chuckled, but didn't make any more comments. They walked on for a while in a companionable silence before he spoke again. "You look very nice today."

"Thank you," she said and considered what to say about her outfit. It was very different from what her twin would wear. "Since I can't wear my heels, I thought I try something a little different." She added that to the list of things she needed to tell Mandy.

"I like it," Phelix said. Leaning over, he whispered in her ear. "But it would be even better if you left your hair down like last Friday night."

A flush rushed over Molly's skin at the suggestion in his voice. She drew in a sharp breath as memories of what they had done on Friday night crashed over her, making desire blossom in her gut. She turned to find a knowing grin slicing across his face. The tension between them broke when he turned his attention to the buildings around them.

"We're here," he said as he led her to the door of a small café.

Molly looked up to find that he'd brought her to one of her favorite places. They had a Reuben that was to die for. After a quick scan of the room, they were lucky enough to find an empty table in the busy lunch crowd.

"So what would you like?" Phelix asked as he plucked the menus from their holder. He handed one to Molly before looking at his.

Scanning over her choices, Molly stared longingly at the Reuben, but skipped over it and moved to the vegan options. What she found there did not whet her appetite. She wrinkled her nose at the mention of tofu before moving on to more palatable fare. "I think I'll have a salad," Molly said, finally decided on the only thing without meat that looked edible.

"Good choice," Phelix agreed. "The fried tofu here doesn't have much flavor." He made a disgusted face that had Molly laughing. When the waiter came around, he ordered the Reuben with extra Thousand Island dressing, just the way Molly liked it.

Pushing away her irritation, she ordered her salad with no bacon, eggs, or cheese. She was going to have to have a long talk with her sister about her diet restrictions. Those were the only things that made a salad worth eating. Slipping her menu back into its holder, she looked up at the smiling face across the table. She was going to have to talk to her sister about more than just her eating habits. This chance meeting was making her life difficult. Phelix was starting to prove that he had the same tastes that she did. If she wasn't careful, she could easily fall in love with him.

"YOU WILL NEVER GUESS WHO SHOWED UP AT MY OFFICE today," Molly grumbled.

Mandy looked up to see her twin coming into her living room. She could tell something was bothering her sister by the way she kicked off her shoes and dropped herself on the couch.

Setting her magazine on her side table, she got up from her seat on the other end of the sofa. "Who?" Mandy asked. She knew her sister didn't drink much, but the woman looked like she could really use one right now.

"Your boyfriend," Molly huffed.

Mandy stopped and looked back to find her sister curled around one of her throw pillows. "What?" She couldn't fathom a reason that Phelix would've stopped by to see Molly. He was an uptown lawyer. What would bring him all the way across town to Molly's medical center?

Molly sighed. "I ran into Phelix in the lobby at lunch time."

Rubbing her tongue against the roof of her

suddenly dry mouth, Mandy turned and made her way into the kitchen. Originally, she was going to just get her sister a drink, but now she needed one too. "What was he doing in the medical center?"

"He was there visiting one of the doctors," Molly explained. "Said he was an old friend."

Pulling out two glasses, Mandy found a bottle of her favorite red wine and worked the cork loose as her sister went on.

"But that's not the part that bothers me."

Mandy stopped and looked out at her sister waiting for her to continue.

"He took me to lunch."

Anger made Mandy freeze, but she pushed it away to finish opening and pouring the wine. She drew in a steadying breath before picking up the glasses and taking them out to her sister. There had to be a good explanation for everything. "Really?" she said trying to sound interested without showing her irritation.

Accepting the glass of wine from her sister, Molly took a gulp before going on. "Yeah. I didn't have much of a choice," she admitted. "The girls in the office abandoned me, and I couldn't think of an appropriate way to turn him down when he asked."

Mandy reclaimed her seat on the couch and thought about it as she sipped her wine. If she had been in Molly's situation, she would have happily abandoned her friends to have lunch with Phelix. She looked over her sister's outfit and wished that Molly had found a way to tell Phelix he had made a mistake, but she understood why her sister didn't. "So what happened?" Mandy was going to have to come up with a convincing cover story for the next time she saw Phelix.

Molly shrugged and cuddled her glass against her, savoring her wine. "I ran into him on our way out to lunch. When he asked why I was there, I told him I was covering for one of the girls in the office."

Mandy considered her sister's story before agreeing. It was an excellent cover story. The fact that there was a lady from her office helping at Molly's made it even more plausible. "So what else happened?" Mandy asked.

"Nothing much," Molly admitted. "We went down the street for lunch and talked."

Jealousy colored Mandy's mood, but she tried not to let it show. Even though they had been going out for a while, she hadn't had much time to sit down and talk with Phelix face to face. While they had spent many hours on the phone, most of their together time was spent doing more physical activities. "What did you talk about?"

"Just stuff," Molly said. She took another drink

before continuing. "Did you know he has a brother?"

"A brother!" Mandy squeaked, nearly dropping her drink. Wiping the sloshed wine from her hand, she continued at a more reasonable level. "No, he hasn't said anything about his family." It was a subject that neither of them had brought up yet.

"He does," Molly explained. "He's got a brother that's a little older than he is." She paused for a second before continuing. "He's a pediatrician."

"Oh, really?" Mandy said. Possibilities raced through her brain. "Maybe we should look him up and see about setting the two of you up." Hooking her sister up with someone else would help to calm the anger the past week had brought up.

Molly laughed.

"So what else did you talk about?" Mandy prompted.

A malevolent smile lit Molly's eyes. "I told him that you had an older sister."

Mandy nearly choked on her wine. She coughed several times before she could breathe again. "You're my twin!" she huffed, outraged that her sister would tell her boyfriend that.

"But I am still older!"

"Yeah, by like two minutes."

"That still makes me older," Molly teased.

Mandy shook her head ignoring the jab. They

had been fighting about that point for as long as she could remember. "So where did you go?" she asked, changing the subject.

"That café down on the corner," Molly answered. "The one with the really good Reubens."

Mandy wrinkled her nose in disgust. "Please tell me you did *not* eat meat in front of him."

"No," Molly reassured her. "I had a salad, and he had the Reuben."

"Good," Mandy said. She paused, recalling the little café. "You should try their fried tofu."

This time Molly wrinkled her nose in disgust. "No, thank you." She shook her head. "I prefer my food to have a flavor of its own."

Molly chuckled at her twin, but sat and listened to Molly's recount of her lunch with Phelix.

"I really had a good time," Molly finally admitted. "I would say this one is a keeper."

Mandy let out a sigh and nodded in agreement. "I know. I plan to hold on to him for as long as I can."

"Good luck," Molly said, and drained the rest of the wine from her glass. She placed the glass on the coffee table as she stood up. "I'm going to go take a bath. It's been a long day."

"Have a good night," Mandy called as her sister left. Sitting on the end of the couch, Mandy stared into her glass and thought about everything her sister had said. It wouldn't have been obvious to anyone else, but Mandy could tell that Molly was developing feelings for Phelix. She could hear it in the rise and fall of Molly's voice and how she told the story.

Draining the rest of the wine from her glass, Mandy got up, collected her sister's glass from the table, and went to clean them out. This situation couldn't be left alone. She was going to have to find a way to keep Molly and Phelix apart.

Three

Molly sighed as she stared through the glass doors at the man leaning against the railing. She'd hoped that yesterday's chance meeting had been a one-time thing, but it was obvious he was waiting for her.

"Good afternoon," Phelix called as soon as she stepped out the door.

Molly's heart flutter at the smile he shot her. Her eyes dropped down his length taking in how well he filled out his dark gray suit. A note of pleasure rippled up her spine. She stamped her foot down on the errant feeling as best she could and smiled back at him. "Hello," she called in greeting. Coming closer, she let him kiss her softly on the lips. "What are you doing here?" she asked when he moved back.

Phelix smiled. "Can't I come take you to lunch?" Reaching his hand out, he brushed a loose strand of hair back from her face. "This is nice."

Embarrassment rushed over Molly's cheeks as she looked away from him. She reached up to touch the loose ends of her hair. She couldn't explain why she had left it down today, but the fact that he noticed made her insides skip with joy. "Thank you," she muttered. Pulling herself together, she met his eyes again. There was something else that she needed to address. "Of course, you can take me to lunch," Molly said. She wanted to yell at him to go away and leave her heart alone, but, she knew if she did, it could cause real problems for her sister. "But, I don't know how long I'll be working here," she warned. "I don't want to trouble you."

Phelix caught her hand and raised it to his lips. "You're worth the trouble."

The flush on Molly's cheeks brightened.

Taking her hand, Phelix wrapped it around his arm to escort her down the street. "Besides, I was already in the area."

"Really?" Molly asked, curious to see why he was in the area. Getting across town at lunch time wasn't an easy feat.

"Nothing serious," Phelix said, waving her concern away. "But it did give me the opportunity to continue our conversation from yesterday." He placed his hand on Molly's lower back and turned her into a different restaurant than the one they had gone to yesterday.

Molly glanced up at the menu board to find her favorite item featured. Joy lifted her up, but her heart dropped when she realized she wouldn't be able to have it. Her sister wouldn't touch the chicken wraps. Even if the mustard sauce they put on them was divine. She turned her attention back to Phelix as they found a table. "I thought we'd covered everything yesterday," she teased, trying not to think about the sandwich she wouldn't be able to have.

His light blue eyes held a hint of amusement. "There is so much that I don't know about you." He held Molly's chair out for her.

"True," Molly agreed as she sat down. A light chuckle slipped out as she thought about the irony of his statement. He'd flip if he knew the truth. "We don't have much of a chance to talk in the evening." Mandy had told her about the last three times she and Phelix had gotten together. They had involved a few of the louder clubs followed by some really passionate session back at his place. That didn't leave a lot of opportunity for heart to heart conversations.

Phelix laughed as he claimed his seat. "No, no we don't." There was something in Phelix's voice that bothered Molly. It was flat, almost bitter, and didn't match the pleasant air he held. Before she could place her finger on what was wrong, he flashed a bright smile and continued in a more eager note. "Well, now that we have a chance to talk, let's not waste it."

Molly smiled. "You hear me talk all the time." She knew how much her sister liked to yammer. "How about I listen to you for a while?"

Surprise slid across Phelix's face. "Sure," he agreed. When the waiter came around, Molly ordered another salad, hold the meat and cheese, while Phelix order the chicken wrap Molly loved so much. Phelix's next words mollified her irritation.

"So what would you like to talk about?" he asked.

Molly thought for a moment before answering. "Tell me about your brother," she encouraged. Mandy's suggestion had passed through Molly's mind a lot during her bath and she was curious to hear what kind of person Phelix's brother was. Was there a possibility of hunting him up to take Phelix's place?

Phelix wrinkled his nose as he picked up his drink. "Why would you want to hear about him?"

A smile slipped across Molly's face. "You can tell a lot about someone by the way they view their family."

Making a noise deep in his throat, Phelix took

a drink before answering. "He's an asshole," he admitted.

"Really?" Molly asked, not believing him.

"Yeah," Phelix went on. "His only redeeming quality is his love for kids. And that only really developed after he went off to college."

Molly raised an eyebrow at him. "So being a doctor isn't a redeeming quality?"

"No," he scoffed. "Anyone can be a doctor."

"But it takes hard work and dedication," Molly said, defending all of the doctors she knew. The job was hard and thankless most of the time.

"So do most professions out there," Phelix said, belittling his brother's work. "It takes years of practice and dedication to get good at any job. Take me, for instance.

"It took me the same number of years to earn my law degree as it did for him to earn his doctorate. We both worked shit jobs for years before we moved up to something better."

Molly considered this as she picked up her drink. Phelix had a point. At one point in her life, Molly had considered becoming a doctor, but quickly found that she wasn't cut out for medical school. She took a sip of her tea while she tried to come up with some kind of response. "So you don't like your brother?"

"I didn't say that," Phelix corrected. "I love my

brother dearly. He's just an asshole."

"Really?" Molly asked again. "How?"

An amused smile turned up the corner of his mouth. "Well," he said with a twinkle in his eye. "He was always doing shit that got me into trouble."

Molly wiggled in her seat, excited to hear his story. "How so?"

The smile on Phelix's face spread. "There was this one time in college. It was exam week," he started, but stopped when the waiter came up with the food.

"I've got a chicken wrap with extra mustard," the waiter said, staring straight at Molly.

Molly gulped as she recognized the guy, praying he didn't say anything. "That's his," she said as she pointed across the table to Phelix.

Confusion crossed the waiter's face, but he placed the wrap down in front of Phelix. "Then you get the salad?" he asked as he placed the salad down for Molly.

"Yes," Molly said.

"Anything else?" the man asked glancing between Molly and Phelix.

"No, thank you," Phelix said.

Nodding, the waiter left.

Molly scooted closer to her meal, picked up her fork, and looked at Phelix just in time to watch him pick up his wrap and take a huge bite. He moaned in pleasure as he licked the mustard off the corner of his mouth.

Anger made her eye twitch as she watched him eat the sandwich that should have been hers.

"This is incredible," Phelix said.

Molly clenched her teeth and stabbed her fork down into her salad. "So what happened with your brother?" she prompted, trying to get him back on subject before she knocked him out and stole his lunch.

"What?" Phelix asked around another mouthful of food.

Forcing a smile to her face, Molly scooped up some salad before answering. "Exam week," she said before sticking the lettuce in her mouth.

"Oh," Phelix said. He took a long drink from his glass. He licked his lips before finishing his story. "It was exam week. I'd just finished the exam for my political science class when my brother shows up on campus with three bottles of tequila."

Molly's eyes widened as he went on.

"Needless to say, I don't remember much about that night, but I do remember the next morning trying to explain to my RA why I had a human skeleton dressed in a serape and sombrero in my dorm room."

Molly nearly choked on her salad. She gulped

down her drink to clear her throat. *"A human skeleton?"*

"Yup," Phelix said. He sounded proud of the stunt. "My brother had snuck in an anatomically correct model of a human skeleton out of his physiology class and set it up in my dorm. I found out later that he'd taken a picture of us doing shots with the thing and plastered them up online. But, I got him back for that one," he said with a snicker.

"Go on."

Phelix chuckled. "I convinced a buddy of mine on the local police force to arrest my brother for abuse of a corpse."

"*What?*" she said, sitting up taller in her chair.

The grin on Phelix's face widened. "I did have photographic evidence to back it up."

Molly nearly snorted her salad. "What happened?"

"My brother got carried out of his boarding house in cuffs and tossed in the back of a police car," Phelix explained. "My friend then drove him around for a while before bringing him back to my dorm where my RA had helped me dress the skeleton up in one of his girlfriend's dresses. We made him apologize to the skeleton and promise never to abuse it again before letting him out of the cuffs."

"No," Molly said, trying not to laugh at the

poor guy's plight.

"Yes," Phelix said. "I think he may still have that thing hanging around in his garage." He picked up his wrap and took another large bite.

"It sounds like you were both horrible people," Molly said as she stirred her salad around.

"True," Phelix answered. "We both gave as good as we got, but we were there for each other when we needed it."

Molly chewed on her lettuce as she thought about Phelix's words. It seemed that Phelix and his brother were similar to her and her sister. There were lots of times they had played horrible pranks on each other, but they had always been there when it counted. "Will you introduce me to your brother?"

Phelix squinted as if he was considering the idea. "Maybe," he said. "But not anytime soon."

Molly's heart sank.

"He's a horn dog and I don't want him nosing in around my girl," Phelix explained. "I may introduce the two of you in a few years."

Trying not to let her disappointment show, Molly agreed and finished her salad. It was getting late and she needed to get back to work.

At the end of lunch, Phelix walked her back to the building and kissed her softly on the lips. "I'll see you tonight," Phelix said as they parted.

Surprise made Molly pause. "Tonight?" she asked, trying to think of what plans she had for the evening.

Phelix gave her a pointed look. "You didn't forget about our date tonight?"

The truth hit Molly like a ton of bricks when she realized what he was talking about. Today was Tuesday. Mandy was supposed to be meeting up with Phelix for dancing at *Vertigo's*. They would probably end the evening back at his house for sex. "Of course not," she said, trying to crush the pain and jealousy blooming in her heart, she gave him the best smile she could manage.

"And make sure to wear those thigh-high stockings," he whispered before turning to go. "We can leave them on this time."

Molly's mouth gaped open, but Phelix was already on his way down the street. Turning, she pushed into the building. His words stung, but there was nothing she could do about it. He was her sister's boyfriend, after all. Molly sighed and pulled out her phone to text her sister. They were going to need to have a talk before Mandy left for her date tonight.

Four

Molly clenched her teeth when she saw Phelix leaning against the railing waiting for her again. Today wasn't going as she'd hoped. She didn't know if she could do this again today.

Yesterday's lunch had caused a big fight between the twins. Mandy had been upset that Molly was meeting Phelix for lunch. In just the few, short meals they had shared, Molly had found out more about her boyfriend than Mandy had in two whole months.

Molly had promptly slapped her sister's jealousy down with a simple threat. All she had to do was tell Phelix the truth. That would put an end to the lunch dates, but, of course, it would also put an end to Mandy's relationship. After much yelling, they decided that Mandy would stop taking her anger out on Molly, while Molly continued to play the part of her sister until they found a way to convince Phelix to stop showing up for lunch. It wasn't the best choice, but it would have to work for now.

Drawing in a deep breath, Molly bit back her irritation and composed herself as she headed out of the building. Forcing joy into her voice, she smiled at the man waiting for her. "Hey, Phelix," she said as he pulled his hand out of his coat pocket and stood up from his perch. She let him kiss her lightly on the lips in greeting. She was going to have to talk to her sister about that too.

"Ready for lunch?" he asked and turned to head up the street. "I know this little place around the corner that's fantastic."

Molly nodded and took the hand he offered. She couldn't help but notice the way their hands fit together. It was too perfect. Shaking the thought away, she pulled her hand from his.

This grabbed Phelix's attention. "Is everything okay?" There was a hint of worry in his voice.

A shiver a dread shot through Molly's heart. Her sister had warned her not to do anything that would make Phelix suspect that they were different people. "Fine," Molly said with a pained smile. She worked her wrist around as if it was stiff. "I twisted my wrist earlier."

Concern filled Phelix's face. "Let me see." Stopping, he took Molly's hand and flexed it around. He rubbed the skin carefully feeling the joint.

The slightest hint of pink crept over Molly's cheeks as she watched his fingers caress her wrist. The way he worked his nimble fingers into her skin reminded her of other things he could do with those digits.

"It looks okay," he mumbled as he flipped her hand over and inspected the inside of her wrist.

"It's fine," Molly said, pulling her hand back and cuddling it against her protectively. The feel of his fingers on her skin was making her inside tighten in ways she didn't want to think about. "I just tried to lift something that was a little too heavy."

Phelix gave her a pointed look and took her hand back. "You should be more careful," he said as he pulled her back into motion. He caressed her hand as they walked. "Joint injuries can give you problems in the future."

Molly nodded, but didn't pull her hand back from his soft touch. She tried to keep the sadness filling her heart from showing on her face. Why couldn't she find a guy as kind and attentive as Phelix was?

As they turned into the local deli, Molly looked around surprise. "I'm vegan," she protested as she looked at the meat-filled counters. Honestly, she loved coming to this place; they had the best pastrami in the area.

"I know," Phelix said in an apologetic voice. "I really wanted a sandwich, but the vegetable soup here is fantastic."

Molly forced the smile on her face not to waver as he ordered her a bowl of soup and the pastrami on rye for himself. She wanted to punch him for picking the food that she would have chosen. Biting back her frustration at her sister's diet, she accepted the soup the cook set on the countertop. Fighting through the lunch rush, Phelix led them to a table to eat.

Phelix held most of the conversation while Molly tried her best to be attentive and pleasant. "Is everything okay?" he asked when a touch of her irritation leaked through.

Forcing her smile back into place, Molly nodded. "Just tired." She tried to cover the frustration she was feeling. The more she found out about Phelix, the more she liked him, and she knew that was a bad thing. She was a starting to have a hard time reminding herself that he was her sister's boyfriend, and she didn't need to screw up their relationship.

"We did get in pretty late last night," Phelix said softly.

Molly nearly let out a sarcastic laugh. She'd expected her sister to have a late night, but having it thrown in her face like that hurt. Trying to keep the disgust from her voice, she nodded. "But we had a really great time," she said coyly as she knew her sister would have. Emotions raced over Phelix's face that threw her off. Was that… anger? She couldn't really tell because he shoved it down under a warm smile before she could identify it.

"Yes," he agreed before checking the time on his watch. "But it's time we get you back to work."

Molly looked up at the clock on the wall and realized that lunch had passed faster than she'd expected.

Phelix cleared their table and walked her back to work without saying anything else.

"You know," Molly said, catching Phelix's attention. "I really do appreciate you taking me out, but you don't have to do it every day." That pained expression passed over his eyes again, but he covered it almost as quickly as it appeared.

Phelix stuck out his lower lip in a cute pout as he drew her into his arms. "I enjoy having lunch with you."

Her heart thumped as his arms settled around her. "I like having lunch with you too," she admitted, "but I know it's got to be a lot of trouble for you to come down here every day."

"I already told you. You're worth the trouble." Phelix raised his hand to her cheek and caressed it softly. "Besides, this gives us an opportunity to get to know each other in new ways."

Molly sighed and smiled at him. How could she be irritated with someone so sweet? "You're right" she finally agreed.

Phelix drew her in for a soft kiss.

Her heart fluttered as he lingered against her lips longer than necessary.

Pulling back, Phelix pushed Molly's loose hair back behind her ear before releasing her. "Have a good day, beautiful."

Reluctantly, Molly turned around and pushed her way into the building. She glanced back to see that he had disappeared into the passing crowd. She hated to see him go, hated the feelings she held for him, and, at the moment, she really hated her sister for being the one that he loved. Pulling out her phone, she sent Mandy a text. If she wanted to keep her boyfriend, Mandy was going to have to do something about these lunchtime visits.

"I DON'T KNOW HOW MUCH MORE OF THIS I CAN TAKE," Molly complained.

Mandy looked at her twin banging around in the kitchen. "Is he doing something wrong?" she asked, watching her sister break eggs into the chocolate powder. The only time Molly made brownies was when she was upset.

"No," Molly fussed, turning the eggs into the mix. "That's the problem." She sighed and looked up at her sister. "If he was a putz, I could handle this, but he's not." Molly banged the mixing bowl on the table for emphases. "He's kind." Bang. "He's considerate." Bang. "He's handsome." Bang. "He's everything I've ever looked for in a guy." Bang! "And he's yours!" *Bang*!

Mandy sat up and considered the fuss her sister was making. It was a good thing Molly was using the metal bowl to make her brownies, but there was no doubt in Mandy's mind that her sister had just dented the hell out of the bottom.

Molly looked up at her twin. "I love you Mandy, and I would never come between you and whoever makes you happy, but this is making me miserable."

Her twin's frustrations made Mandy's heart hurt. "I'm sorry," she apologized. She stared at her sister for a long minute. "How can I help?" she finally asked.

Molly wacked the mix with the spoon she was using to stir it. "Talk to him."

Mandy sighed.

"I've tried to convince him to stop coming by telling him that I didn't want to trouble him, but he told me that I was..." Molly paused and corrected her wording. "You were worth the trouble."

"That's so sweet," Mandy gushed.

Shaking her head, Molly poured the beaten batter into the pan. "For the last three days, he has taken me out to all of my favorite dives around work. And do you know what I have eaten there?" She paused and shot her sister an accusing look.

"Salads," Mandy said sheepishly

"Salads!" Molly yanked the oven open and slammed the pan onto the top shelf of the oven. "And while I am eating crunchy water, he orders my favorite foods."

Mandy laughed, earning her a sharp glare.

"He even got extra mustard on the pastrami!"

Mandy's mirth increased as she took in the torture her sister had endured. "That explains the empty carton." She pointed to the deli box sitting on the counter.

Sighing, Molly moved the empty container to the trash can. "I had to go back after work and get a sandwich," she confessed. "I can't live on just veggies."

Mandy's laughter earned her another glare. "Yes you can," she said as she wiped tears from her eye. "They're better for you than meat. Besides, I do it."

Molly just shook her head again. "Look, just

convince your boyfriend to stop coming by during lunch." She dropped the dirty dishes in the sink and yanked the tap on. "Or stopped being vegan so I can get a decent meal during the day."

Mandy chuckled. "I'll see what I can do." She grinned at her twin.

"Thank you," Molly said. She sighed again and slammed the tap closed.

"So tell me about these dates you have been having with my boyfriend." Mandy wiggled in her chair ready to hear all about the delicious stories that Phelix had been sharing.

Letting out another frustrated breath, Molly shook her head and repeated some of the funnier bits from their lunches.

Five

THURSDAY, MOLLY STEPPED OUT ONTO THE STREET AND looked around for Phelix. A wave of disappointment swept through her when she found he wasn't there. Shaking her head, she turned up the street to the bakery on the corner. Thoughts of the missing man floated around her skull, and she considered her feeling as she walked. She should be happy that Mandy had finally convinced him to stop coming by, but she wasn't. Even though she knew he was Mandy's boyfriend, she couldn't help the fact that she enjoyed his company. He always had something to say to make her smile.

Molly pushed the door to the bakery open and joined the line. Looking around, she studied the crowd of people in the shop as she waited. She caught herself checking the faces of the men to see if Phelix was among them. Shaking her head again, she stepped up to the counter to order two of the meat buns that this place was so famous for.

At least today she would be able to enjoy something that she actually liked. Molly sighed loudly when the baker handed over her bag. She decided that the best thing to do was to go back to her desk and eat there. In just the few short days that Phelix had been stopping by, she had gotten used to his company and sitting in the shop alone didn't sound very appealing. Molly pressed her lips into a hard line and schooled her thought back to where they should be. Phelix was taken, and she did not need to be lusting after her sister's man. She glanced around the street one last time before going into her building. Obviously, whatever Molly had said last night had finally put an end to her lunch time dates.

Six

Molly laughed as she stared out the front doors of her building on Friday. Phelix looked good leaning against the railing waiting for her. He had one hand stuck in the pocket of his dark-blue, suit pants and was relaxed back with his ankles crossed. He glanced up as soon as Molly stepped out of the building.

Phelix smiled, pushing up into a more respectable position. "Hey there, beautiful."

She smiled back as he leaned forward and kissed her softly.

When he pulled back, he lifted a single red rose up between them and spun it.

"What's this for?" she asked, taking the offered flower.

"It's an apology," he explained. "I don't know what I did on Wednesday to upset you, but I'm sorry."

Molly chuckled as she studied the rose. She

knew she shouldn't be, but she was happy that he was back today. Yesterday's lunch had been rather banal. "You didn't do anything on Wednesday." Molly smiled and smelled the flower. "I was just tired."

Phelix made an odd noise. "Then consider it an apology for missing lunch with you yesterday." He placed his hand on Molly's lower back and steered her off to find food. "I got called away for an emergency, and couldn't make it back in time to take you to lunch."

Molly laughed. "You don't have to take me to lunch every day." She sighed. Her better judgment was starting to overcome the joy she got from seeing him waiting for her. "I know how much of a pain it is to get across town at lunch time." Molly looked up at Phelix. She was surprised to see a tightness around his eyes. Was that irritation? Why had her words upset him?

"It's no trouble at all." Phelix's smile replaced whatever other emotion was showing in the corners of his eyes. "I enjoy having lunch with you. It brightens my day." By the time he had finished his words, the irritation was gone.

"Thank you." Molly looked down shyly. "To be honest, I really did miss you yesterday." She tensed as she realized what she had just said. "But you really shouldn't go through the trouble."

Molly amended her statement. She was supposed to be convincing Phelix to stop coming by during the day. Not encouraging him.

"You're so sweet." Phelix kissed the hair at her temple. "Now let's get you something to eat." He held open a door for her.

Molly chuckled as they went in to order. It looked like today was going to be another salad day. She smiled and spun the rose in her fingers. To spend time with someone as sweet as Phelix, maybe she could learn to be vegan.

"SO I TALKED WITH PHELIX ABOUT HIS LUNCHTIME VISITS." Mandy handed her twin a glass of wine.

Molly tucked her feet up on her sister's couch and listened. "What did he say?"

Mandy watched as her sister sat quietly on her couch. There was something about the way she held herself that showed her unease. Mandy hoped she was reading more into her sister's posture than was there. "He apologized for bothering me and said that he would stop."

Molly took a long pull of the wine and rolled it around in her mouth before swallowing.

Mandy could see the wheels in her twin's mind turning and tracked the woman's thoughts as she processed them. The fact that her twin didn't seem happy about the news made Mandy's heart skip. Has something else happened between them?

"So that means I can get back to my regular routine," Molly finally answered.

The smile that graced her twin's lips looked a little too forced for Molly's liking, but she nodded her head, hoping she was just being paranoid. "Yup. No more annoying guy to bother you." Mandy paused for a moment and considered the question that had plagued her all day. She wasn't sure she wanted to know the answer, but she was dying to ask. She studied the liquid inside her wine glass hoping the question would sound nonchalant. "Did he stop by again today?" She glanced up at her sister just in time to catch her nod.

"Yes. And he brought an apology."

Anger bubbled in Mandy's stomach, but she clenched her teeth against letting it out and took a sip of her wine. She wanted to lash out, but she knew her sister didn't deserve her anger. It was Phelix who was causing the problem. After cooling her temper, she turned to look at her sister. "An apology?" she asked, trying to keep her cool

"Apparently he thought he upset me on Wednesday and brought me a rose. I left it upstairs in a vase if you want it."

A note of jealousy raced through Mandy. Although they had spent plenty of time together, this was the first rose she'd gotten from Phelix. The fact that he presented it to her sister burned her up. Mandy took several breaths to get a leash on her temper. As the rage cooled, she thought about her sister's words. Something didn't fit. If he'd upset Molly on Wednesday, then why did he wait until Friday to apologize when he saw her on Thursday night? "That's odd," she said voicing her thought, "he didn't say anything about it when I saw him on Thursday." Mandy cocked her head and recalled her evening with Phelix. "Why was he apologizing?"

"Wednesday was not a good day, and I was mad that he'd showed up." Molly paused and gave her sister a pointed look. "That man is very perceptive. We should tell him what's going on before he figures it out."

"No," Mandy snapped. Telling him would surely end their relations, and she wasn't ready for that. "He doesn't need to know." She was sure she could find a way to get them out of this if she could just convince Phelix to stop showing up for the lunchtime visits with her sister.

Molly shrugged before continuing. "He also said the apology was for not showing up on Thursday afternoon. Something about an emergency."

That threw Mandy for another loop. What kind

of emergency did lawyers have? Phelix hadn't mentioned that during their date either. "Maybe he's just overworked," she said, shrugging it off. "You know how lawyers can get." He had been spending a lot of extra time at the office trying to get a case together.

"That must be it," Molly agreed. "So tell me about this trip you're taking next weekend."

"It's going to be great!" Mandy gushed, glad her sister had asked. She was done dwelling on the issues with her boyfriend for now. "A friend got us into a Shoshoni Yoga retreat. It's going to be an entire weekend of relaxation and yoga. Nothing to think about but me and resting." She paused and considered her sister. Mandy could see the stress from this last week on her sister. "Are you sure you don't want to come? I could still get you in."

Molly chuckled. "Not my thing." She shook her head. "Give me a good book and a hot bath, and I'll be good."

Mandy agreed and proceeded to ramble on about the upcoming trip. She really needed this time to relieve her stress. She'd talk to Phelix again this weekend and make sure he understood that she didn't want him stopping by for lunch.

Seven

"What are you doing here?" Molly asked as she stepped out of the building to get lunch. Her heart skipped with both joy and anger as she walked over to Phelix leaning on the railing with his hands in his pocket. She'd spent the entire weekend wrestling with her emotions and coming to terms with the fact that she wouldn't see him again.

Phelix just smiled. "Waiting for you." He leaned forward and gave her a welcoming kiss.

Molly laughed. "I thought you said that you wouldn't be coming for lunch anymore."

"I know," he said as he took her arm. "But, I missed you."

She chuckled at his nonchalant attitude to breaking his promise. "We spent most of the weekend together," she pointed out, knowing her sister hadn't been home either Friday or Saturday. The only reason Molly hadn't called the cops was a drunken text she received saying her twin was out with Phelix. Molly had tried to cool the jealousy that stole over her in a long bath, but had to resort to a pint of ice cream to kill her emotions.

Phelix just shrugged again. "What can I say?" he added with a campy smile, "I can't get enough of you."

Molly laughed again. "Come on," she said, leading him down the street, "Let me buy your lunch."

Phelix cocked an eyebrow. "I thought it was the man's job to treat a lady."

His chivalry touched her heart. "Maybe in the past," she said, trying to suppress the goofy smile on her face. "But these are modern times. You bought lunch all last week, this week it's my treat."

Phelix wrapped his arm around Molly's shoulder and pulled her against his side. "Oh no," he said. "It wouldn't be proper if I let you do that." He kissed her temple. "Besides, I didn't pay for you all week."

Molly scoffed at him, but didn't pull away from his embrace. She loved the feel of him close to her. "You only missed one day," she huffed. "And what about the weekend?" She was pretty sure that he'd paid for whatever her sister all weekend.

"That's different," Phelix whispered into her hair.

Molly shivered at the tone of his voice. There

was something almost angry about it. Glancing up, she tried to gauge his reaction. His eyes were darker than usual, and they held something that she didn't understand.

Stopping short, Phelix pulled her around to face him. Trapping her in his arms, he pressed a kiss to her lips that left her weak in the knees.

Molly couldn't help but melt into the passion burning from him. When they parted for air, it took Molly a moment to catch her breath. Her heart raced as desire and longing filled her deep inside.

"I can't wait to get you back in my bed," Phelix whispered. He wrapped his hand around the back of her head and pulled her in, so her cheek rested against his chest.

Shocked by this sudden outpouring of emotion, Molly stood there dumbfounded and listened to his heartbeat while the people on the sidewalk flowed around them. Her hands caressed the material of his coat feeling the muscles under them.

"The scratches are all healed up," he said softly into her hair.

Remembering the feel of his bare skin under her fingers, embarrassment rushed over her skin. She pushed back from him. "Um... I'm sorry about that." Molly turned away to hide the red on her face.

Phelix laughed and pulled her to him again.

"Don't be." He kissed her again. When he moved back, he caressed her cheek with his thumb. "It was a really special night for me."

Molly's heart leaped and she could feel the first vestiges of tears pricking at the corners of her eyes. Turning her face away from his hand, she closed her eyes to fight down her feelings. She was sure he and her sister had sex many times since then. It made no sense why that one night would have been special to him. Taking a cleansing breath, she looked back up at him with a smile she really didn't feel. "Come on." She nodded her head, pointing down the street where the café was waiting for them. "Let's go get lunch before it's too late." She worked to keep the pain she felt from showing in her voice.

Phelix stared at her for a moment longer before releasing her. "All right." He took her hand and caressed the back with this thumb. "But I'm buying today."

Molly chuckled. "Fine, but I get lunch tomorrow." She shot him a sidelong look.

Phelix gave her a mischievous smile. "All right," he said, giving in. "You can get lunch tomorrow."

Molly wasn't sure what was up, but she had a sneaking suspicion that she wouldn't be paying for lunch tomorrow either.

Eight

A smile crept across Molly's face as she came out to find Phelix waiting in his usual spot on Tuesday. There was a rather large basket next to him that piqued her curiosity.

"Good afternoon, beautiful," Phelix said and greeted her with his normal, soft kiss. "Ready for lunch?" he asked as he picked up the basket.

Molly cocked an eyebrow at the wicker box. "What's that?" she asked as he took her hand and led her to the corner.

He smiled smugly. "Lunch."

Sticking her bottom lip out, she pouted playfully at him. "*I* was supposed to buy lunch today," she complained in a teasing fashion.

Phelix pulled her against his side for a hug as they crossed the street. "I thought a picnic would be a nice change." He led the way down the street to the little park.

Molly smiled at his deviousness. "Fine," she

huffed. "But I'm getting lunch tomorrow."

Phelix kissed the side of her head again, but didn't say anything.

Molly let out a short sigh. She was starting to really like those little kisses.

"All right," Phelix finally agreed. Guiding her over to the large fountain in the middle of the park, he set his burden on the ledge around the pool and placed Molly next to it. He flipped the lid back to reveal several lacquered boxes. "I hope you can use chopsticks." Lifting a box out, he set it into her hands and added a pair of polished chopsticks to the top of the box.

Molly could not recall if her sister could use chopsticks, but figured it really didn't matter. She set the box in her lap and fitted the sticks to her hand. "Of course," she said as she clicked the sticks at Phelix.

Laughing, he took the other two boxes out. Retrieving two bottles from the basket, he flipped the top shut. He set the two boxes on top of basket and popped the top open on the largest one to show four lines of sushi. There were some slivers of pickled ginger and a dab of wasabi in the little cups built into the side of the box.

Molly laughed in joy and surprise. She loved sushi.

Phelix pulled the lid off the soy sauce. "I'm

sorry these aren't exactly freshly made, but they are vegan, so it shouldn't make a difference."

"Did you make these?" Molly took off the top of her bento box and looked in at the rice and mixed veggies.

"The bento, yes, but sadly, I got the sushi from *Wasabi* on 25th," Phelix admitted as he handed one of the bottles over to her. "I hope you don't mind oolong tea."

"That's fine," Molly said, accepted the bottle and opened it. She took a drink of the amber colored liquid. "This was very thoughtful of you."

Phelix smiled in response. "Anything for you, beautiful." He picked up his chopsticks and dug into his box.

Molly smiled again and looked at her food again. "*Itadakimasu,*" she said, and picked up her meal.

Phelix chuckled at her.

"What?" she huffed as she caught up a bit of rice. "I like Japanese." She stuck the bite in her mouth to enjoy his work.

Phelix's grin widened as he worked on his own lunch. "Somehow, I knew you would."

Molly searched her brain to see if her sister had ever mentioned anything about Phelix taking her to a Japanese restaurant. She couldn't think of one, and Mandy had a really bad habit of telling

Molly everything that they did together. Especially after Phelix had started stopping by for lunch.

"So what are you going to do this weekend?" she asked as she ate.

A confused look crossed Phelix's face.

"While I'm away at the Shoshoin retreat."

The confusion changed to surprise.

"You forgot about the retreat," Molly said flatly.

Phelix laughed. "I guess I had." He rubbed his hand into the back of his neck slightly embarrassed.

Shaking her head, Molly turned back to her food waiting for him to think about his answer.

"I guess I'll be looking forward to Monday when I can see you again," Phelix said with a wry grin. "When do you leave?"

Molly was sure Mandy had told him all about it, but she decided it would be a good idea to remind him. That way he could save a little face with her sister. "Thursday evening shortly after work," Molly informed him.

Phelix nodded his head and went back to his food. "That means two more lunches before you leave for the weekend." He sounded a little sad at losing that last lunchtime.

"Hey," Molly said, reaching across the basket she patted his shoulder. "Don't be upset. I'll see you tonight." Her insides twisted as she thought about her sisters standing date with this man. The smile that crossed Phelix's face was definitely bitter.

"Yeah, that's true," he said and turned back to his food.

They ate in silence for a while as Molly pondered his reaction. He'd told her yesterday that he was looking forward to getting her back into bed, but that idea put him off today. Okay, it was her sister that was going to get into his bed tonight, but he didn't know that. Molly sighed as a hint of melancholy slipped into her mood. She looked down at the food she had been eating. It no longer tasted good. She slipped the top back on the part that she hadn't finished. "Thank you for lunch," she said as she smiled up at Phelix. "It was very good."

Concern crossed his face. "Are you done already?" he asked as he glanced at the untouched sushi on the basket.

"I'm not very hungry right now," Molly admitted.

Phelix gave her an evaluating glance. "Are you feeling all right?"

Molly shrugged, not really commenting on it. She'd felt a little off today, but she blamed it on the rather large pile of folders someone had left on her desk this morning. "Yeah, I'm fine," she said, trying to ease his worries. "I think I'm just a little tired." She tried to hand the bento box back to him.

"Why don't you take that with you?" he suggested. "You can eat it when you get hungry."

Gratitude washed over her. "Thank you." She rested the box in her lap as Phelix cleaned up what was left of their lunch. "I'm sorry for cutting lunch short," she said as she rubbed the golden leaves painted on the black box.

Phelix reached over and placed his hand on her cheek. "Don't worry about it."

Molly leaned into his hand, enjoying the feel of his warm fingers against her.

"Just make sure you get some good rest tonight," he said, caressing her skin with his thumb.

Her heart jumped and she opened her eyes. "Does that mean you're canceling our date?" she asked hoping she had misheard what he said. Mandy was going to be super mad if she had just messed up her sister's evening.

"Not if you're feeling better by this evening," Phelix said. There was a note of concern in his voice.

Molly let out a weak laugh that was tinged with both relief and jealousy. "Don't worry, I will definitely be better by this evening," she said, trying to keep the bitter notes out of her voice. Her sister would be perfectly fine this evening.

Phelix gave her a long look before kissing her lightly on the forehead. "Just don't push yourself." Standing up, he lifted the basket and held his hand out for Molly to take.

She let him help her to her feet. "I won't," she promised.

Phelix cuddled her against his side as they walked back to the medical offices.

"I'll have this back to you soon." Molly held the box up as they closed on her building.

"Take your time and enjoy it," Phelix said before kissing her temple again. "Thank you for a wonderful time."

"I'll see you later, then." Molly leaned up and kissed him on the cheek.

A surprised look flashed across Phelix's face.

Molly quickly scanned her memories to see if she had just done something her sister wouldn't have, but she relaxed when a lopsided grin spread replaced the surprise.

"Yes, I'll see you later." He petted her hair back from her face before letting her go inside and back to work.

Molly pulled out her cell phone to send her sister a text message. This was definitely something that Mandy needed to know before Phelix showed up tonight for their date.

Nine

"HEY, BEAUTIFUL," PHELIX CALLED.

Molly looked up at the man waiting for her and let out a soft snort. He was the last person she wanted to see right now. Looking back down, she continued out the door to meet him.

He paused and cocked his head. "Are you feeling okay?' he asked as he stepped toward her.

She turned her face away before he could give her his normal greeting kiss. "I'm fine," she lied. "I just have a bit of a headache." In honesty, she'd felt horrible. The day started out bad and had slowly been sliding down hill since. She was ready to call it a day and go lay down, but she had to finish the pile of files on her desk first.

Phelix gave her an incredulous look, but let the fib slide. Reaching out he took her by the upper arms and pulled her in against him.

Molly laid her head against his chest and relaxed in his comforting hold.

"Is there anything I can do?" he asked, nuzzling her hair.

"Not really," Molly answered. She'd woken up this morning with body aches and the beginning signs of a cold. A healthy dose of vitamin C and Echinacea had gotten her on her feet, but all she really wanted was some rest. The daytime cold medication she had taken wasn't making things any easier either. Her vision swam in and out of focus and her head felt like someone had filled it with helium and it was about to float away. Placing her hands against his chest, she pushed away from him. "Let's just get something to eat." She prayed that food would help to dilute the medication so she could get through the rest of her day.

Phelix held her by the upper arms for a moment. "Maybe you should go home," he suggested. "Some rest might make you feel better."

Molly sighed. She knew he was right, but she still had a lot of stuff to do before she could call it a day. She stepped out of his hold. "I'll be okay," she said, brushing his concern away. "I just need food." She turned and started up the street. "I still have a lot of stuff to do before the end of the week."

Phelix fell into step beside her. "You're trip isn't going to be very much fun if you push yourself to hard and get sick," he pointed out as he wrapped his arm around her shoulders and drew her close.

Molly clenched her teeth as she remembered her sister's upcoming trip. Mandy was supposed to leave tomorrow. "It'll be all right," she reassured him. "I just need to get some rest before I go."

"All right," Phelix reluctantly agreed.

Tears burned at the corners of Molly's eyes. She was touched that he both cared about how she was feeling and had enough good sense not to argue with her about it. She leaned into his side and let him lead the way down the street to the deli. When he pulled out a chair, she gladly sat in it.

"Wait here while I get you something," he said before disappearing to the counter.

A weak grin stole across her face. She was supposed to be buying lunch today. She glanced up when he set the bowl down in front of her. "Today was my day to get lunch," she protested.

"Shh," he hushed her as he took the seat next to her. "Don't worry about that right now. Just eat your soup and feel better."

Molly smiled and looked down at the bowl of steaming vegetable soup. "Thanks," she said as she picked up the spoon and stirred her food. "I'll get lunch next time. Promise."

Phelix rubbed the back of her neck. "I'm not worried about it, beautiful."

Molly closed her eyes and enjoyed the feel of his fingers on her neck. The gentle touch was just enough to take the edge off her headache.

His fingers pulled away from her neck as he spoke. "Eat your soup."

Opening her eyes, she looked down into the bowl of vegetables. She stirred them around for a moment before lifting the first bite to her mouth. A warm plume of steam brushed against her face. The smell hit her, turning her stomach and making her stop. She dropped the spoon back into her bowl untasted. "I don't think I can do this," she said trying to suppress the nausea swelling inside her. Drawing a measured breath in through her mouth, she pushed the bowl away and hung her head.

Phelix wrapped his arm around her, pulling her against him. "It's okay, baby," he cooed soothingly.

Molly buried her face in the crook of his neck.

He held her for a moment before slipping his free hand up to the back of her neck.

His cool hand felt good against her skin.

Sitting her up, he raised his hand to her forehead. Concern crossed his face as he flipped his hand over and rested the back against her cheek. "Come on." Standing up, he pulled Molly to her feet before touching his food. "You've got a fever.

I'm taking you home."

Molly looked at the two meals left untouched on the table. "But your lunch…"

"That's not important," he said, guiding her away from the table and back out into the street. "Getting you home is."

"I'm okay," she tried to argue as he took her back down the street to her building. "Really, it's not that bad."

Ignoring her protests, Phelix hit the button on the elevator and waited for the car.

A wave of dizziness came over her and she leaned against him for support. His arms closed around her and she let out a resigned sigh. There was no point in trying to argue with him when they both could tell she wasn't doing well. Giving in, she closed her eyes, trusting that he would take care of her.

A smile turned her mouth as she thought about the mess this would make in her office. Her co-workers were already teasing her about the hot guy that had been taken her to lunch lately. What were they going to say when he showed up to take her home while she was sick? At least, she wouldn't have to explain anything right away. Since it was lunch time, most of the girls would be out of the office.

When the elevator arrived, Phelix led her in,

leaned against the wall next to the control panel, and supported her against him "What floor?"

Reaching out, Molly poked the button for the administrative section.

His hand slid up and down Molly's back soothing her aches as the elevator set itself into motion. When the door opened again, he helped her out into the hall.

Turning to the left, Molly led the way down to her office.

Phelix's hand made it to the door before Molly could pull it open. He held it open as they went inside.

"Molly?"

Molly cringed at the sound of her real name. She looked up to see Beth, her desk mate, was still there manning the phones while the rest of the office had gone out.

Beth stood up from her desk and took a tentative step toward them. "Are you all right?"

"No. She's not," Phelix answered before Molly could. He pulled out a chair and placed her in it.

Molly leaned against the desk and watched through half-lidded eyes as he hooked the trash can out from under the desk and set it close to her. She tried to smile at his thoughtfulness, but the rolling of her stomach kept her from enjoying his caring gesture. She felt rather green.

"Is your boss around?" Phelix asked.

"Yeah, let me get him."

Looking up, Molly watched as Beth disappeared into the depths of the billing office. The warm pressure of Phelix's hand on the back of her neck eased the pain from her head as they waited.

"It'll be okay," he whispered.

A hit of worry added to the uncomfortable feeling in her stomach. Beth had used Molly's real name when they came in. There was no way that Phelix could have missed it. She would have to think of a plausible excuse for that one, but coming up with one could wait until the pounding in her head stopped.

"Are you all right, Molly?"

Molly cringed as her boss used her real name again. She could feel Mr. Baker's evaluating gaze brush over her. The sick in her stomach made opening her mouth a bad idea, so she shook her head gently without looking up.

"She's running a fever and needs to go home," Phelix informed her boss.

There was something in his authoritative tone that made Molly glance up at him. In that instance, he was not the kind man she knew. His posture demanded respect and attention. She dropped her head back down as she heard her boss respond to him.

"Fairlane?"

Molly didn't look up to see Phelix's response, but she felt his hand tense on the back of her neck as he responded.

"Of course," Mr. Baker said. "If you think she needs to go home."

"I do," Phelix answered.

Shock brought her face up to look at her boss. She didn't understand how Phelix had convinced her boss to let her leave so easily; he was usually such a hard ass about finishing work before leaving. She stared at him wondering if she really looked that bad.

Mr. Baker knelt down so that he was closer to Molly's level. "Is there someone that we can call to come get you?"

"That won't be necessary," Phelix refused the offer before she could answer. "I'll make sure she gets home."

Mr. Baker looked up at him. "Are you sure?" he asked. "I know you're busy."

"It will be fine," Phelix reassured him. "Can I use your phone?"

"It's on the desk."

Pulling his hand away from her neck, he picked up one of the phones on the desk.

Molly watched as he held the phone to his ear and waited. Their eyes met for a brief moment before he looked away. Confusion raced through Molly's mind. She could have been mistaken, but she thought she saw guilt in his eyes, but she didn't know what he should be remorseful for.

"Hey Heather, it's me," he said as he turned his back to Molly. "Something has come up at lunch and I'm going to be a little late getting back." He paused, listening to a voice that Molly couldn't hear. "Yes, I know I have appointments, but this is important. It won't take long." He paused again. "Thanks, Heather." Phelix dropped the phone back to the cradle and turned to face Molly again. "Come on," he said as he took her arm and gently pulled her into motion.

Molly moaned as her stomach protested the moment.

"Here's her bag," Beth said as she handed Molly's things to Phelix.

He nodded his thanks and pulled the satchel over his shoulder.

"Let me know if you need anything," Mr. Baker said as he followed them to the office door.

"I will," Phelix answered as they left.

Molly leaned on him heavily. The world was moving in funny directions now that she was standing again.

"Come on, beautiful, you can do this," he encouraged to keep her moving.

Nodding, Molly tried to stand up a little straighter. It didn't work very well.

Once they were back in the elevator, Phelix let her lean against him again.

"How does my boss know you?" Molly asked as her addled mind turned the entire scene over in her head.

"I told you. I know people here," Phelix said as he rubbed her upper back.

There was something about that statement that bothered Molly, but she let it go. She chalked it up to his claim of knowing a doctor in the building. Perhaps he handled some of their malpractice cases, but that didn't explain why her boss had let her go on just his word. She let it go for now. There would be plenty of time to think about it later. "You really don't have to take me home," she protested. "I can call my sis…" She paused before she could bring up her sister. She didn't want to risk him wanting to wait around for Mandy to come. That would be very bad. "I could call someone to come get me."

Phelix patted her on the back. "I would feel better seeing you home myself."

Unable to think of any other reason to refuse, Molly nodded in agreement.

Guiding her out of the building, Phelix waved down a cab. He loaded her into it and gave her address to the driver.

Molly sighed and shook her head. She felt horrible for making him take her home in a cab.

"Just relax," Phelix said as he pressed her head to his shoulder. "I'll have you home shortly."

Letting everything go, Molly closed her eyes and listened to his heartbeat. She was almost asleep by the time they had gotten her back to her apartment building.

Phelix's gentle prodding brought Molly back from the edge of sleep. "Come on," he said softly as he coaxed her from the car.

"Thanks," Molly said as she let him help her out. "I can get home from here. You should get back to work."

"Nonsense," Phelix said as he shut the car door and sent the cab off. "You're in no condition to take care of yourself right now." He placed his hand on Molly's shoulder to steady her. "I have time to see you to bed before I have to get back," he insisted.

Molly clutched him as he carefully lifted her from her feet. The sudden motion made her head spin and she slouched over in his arms. "I'm sorry," she groaned.

"Shh," he soothed as he headed inside. "It will be okay."

Molly relaxed and trusted that he would take

care of her. Her heart skipped for a moment as they mounted the step and she feared he would take her to her sister's apartment, but they passed up the second floor without a pause.

"Where are your keys?" Phelix asked as he set her down in front of her door.

"Here," Molly said as she fished in her bag for her keys. She opened the door and led the way in. She turned to stop Phelix from coming in. "Thank you," she said, hoping he would take the hint. "I'm good now."

Phelix shook his head. "All the way to bed," he insisted as he crowded her into the room and shut the door behind him.

Unable to drag up the energy to fight with him, she dropped her keys on the coffee table and headed into her room. She was both horrified and delighted that he was there. Her sister was going to go nuts when she found out the Phelix brought her home, but the fact that he cared enough to put her to bed warmed her heart. She was already starting to fall for the guy, but this was going to push her over the edge.

Letting out a long sigh, she pushed those thoughts from her mind. Turning around she sat on the edge of her bed and kicked off her shoes.

"I know you haven't eaten anything, but here."

Molly looked up to see Phelix coming in with

a glass of water.

"What is it?" she asked as she held out her hand.

He placed two white pills in her palm. "Something for the fever."

She looked at the pills and swallowed hard. Just the thought of taking them turned her stomach. She shook her head and tried to hand them back.

Phelix caught her hand and pushed it toward her. "I know you don't feel good, but try," Phelix begged. He gave her the biggest puppy dog eyes he could. "Please."

Molly drew in a deep breath, then slowly let it out and took the glass of water so she could take the pills.

"That's my girl," Phelix encouraged as he waited for her to take them.

Molly glared at him for a second before popping the pills in her mouth and washing them down. She shivered with disgust, but the liquid and pills seemed to stay down for the moment.

"That's it," Phelix said as he took the glass back. He caught Molly's hand and kissed the back of her fingers. "Now let's get you to bed."

A halfhearted smile cut across Molly's face as she watched Phelix take the glass over to her side table. This was probably the same bug that kept her sister from the date with Phelix a week ago.

Mandy had been so afraid of Phelix coming over and seeing her while she was a mess. Had Mandy known he was so tender, she might have called him up and things would have been very different now.

The irony of the situation pulled a light chuckle from her, and she immediately regretted it as her stomach rolled. Slapping her hand over her mouth, Molly bolted from the edge of the bed toward the bathroom as her body rejected the water and pills. She made it to the toilet as the first convulsion pushed the contents of her stomach up. Fingers pulled her hair away from her face as the first bout of retching subsided. A gentle hand rubbed her back as Phelix held her hair out of danger's way. Tears prickled at her eyes as the stomach spasms drove her into dry heaves. "I'm sorry," she cried and leaned her head over onto her arm. Embarrassment pushed more tears from her eyes.

"It's all right," Phelix soothed her. He rubbed little circles into her back before reaching up and grabbing the hand towel from the wall. Twisting on the water in the sink, he soaked one end of the cloth in cold water before bringing it down to wipe Molly's face. Setting the towel down, she gathered up her glass and pressed it to her lips. "Just rinse your mouth out."

Nodding, Molly sat up and sipped at the water. She swished it around and spat it out before reaching up to flush away the mess.

Phelix slipped a hand under her arm and helped her off the floor. "Let's get you to bed."

She leaned on him heavily as he guided her into her bedroom.

Holding her up, he folded back the covers and helped her to sit on the edge of the bed.

Molly turned to arrange her bedding but didn't have the chance to get in before Phelix drew her attention again.

"Do you have something to sleep in?" he asked. Turning around he went to her dresser and pulled the top drawer open.

The fact that he paused and stared down into her drawer of unmentionables amused Molly. "Third drawer," she called.

"Thanks," Phelix called and slid the top drawer shut. Pulling the third drawer open, he started rummaging through it.

Molly clutched at her upset stomach and watched as he searched through her night clothing and wondered what he was going to find. There were some rather provocative things in that drawer. She prayed he had the good sense not to bring her anything lacy or strappy. She let out a little sigh of relief when he pulled out an oversized sleep shirt.

"Let's get you changed," Phelix brought the shirt over and shook it out.

Slowly, Molly worked the buttons on her shirt loose. She stopped just before pulling the material open and looked up at her companion. She felt weird changing in front of her sister's boyfriend, but she couldn't think of a good way to make him leave that wasn't rude. She chewed on her lip for a moment as she considered her issue. The whole idea of privacy was about preserving her dignity, but she'd lost that while she barfed. Besides, she didn't have anything he hadn't already seen. Giving in to the inevitable, she pulled her blouse off and dropped it to the floor. Her bra followed shortly after. She stood up to strip out of her skirt, but paused as Phelix held up the shirt. She smiled weakly and let him slip the loose top down over her head. His fingers trailed along her back as he guided the material over her bare skin.

"Even sick, you're still beautiful," Phelix said as ran his hand over the skin on Molly's upper arm that the short-sleeve sleep shirt had left bare.

"Flatterer," Molly teased.

Phelix chuckled. "Only when it's deserved." He shot her a cheeky grin.

Molly gave him a more sincere smile before working the zipper on her skirt down. She dropped the confining clothing to the floor with the rest of her things. For a moment, she considered taking off her stockings but decided that they weren't annoying enough to bother with. Giving up, she climbed in bed and moved to a comfortable position.

Phelix pulled the covers over her and tucked her in. "I really hate this, but I can't stay," he sighed as he patted the blanket over her. "Is there anything you need before I leave?"

Molly glanced around and found a glass of water and trash can near her bed. Those would go a long way to solving half of her problem. There was only one thing missing. "My phone," she said. Once Phelix was gone, she was going to have to let her sister know what was going on.

"Where is it?" Phelix asked as went to find the missing device.

"In my bag," she called.

After a few minutes, Phelix came back in with her phone in his hand. He tapped in a number and let the phone ring once before hanging up. "Here," he said as he handed the phone over. "Call me if you need me."

Molly looked at the new number slightly confused. Didn't Mandy already have his phone number? She gave him questioning eyes, but he didn't explain.

Leaning over, he kissed her temple. "I have to go now," he said. "Get some rest. I'll be back to check on you later, beautiful." Phelix patted her hip one last time before leaving.

Staring at the door he had just barely closed, Molly listened as he made his way through her apartment and out the front door. She relaxed in the bed and tried to sort through her swirling thoughts. Until this point, she and her twin had been very careful about holding up the illusion that they were one person, but she wasn't sure how long that lie was going to last.

She closed her eyes and thought back over the day. There was no way he could have missed her coworkers calling her by her real name, but why hadn't he asked about it? And why had he given her a new number? Molly rubbed the edge of her phone as she thought, but couldn't come up with an answer. She was going to have to get together with her sister and figure out what to do.

Opening her eyes, she pulled up her message screen and dropped her sister a quick note on what had happened. They needed to have a long talk. It was time they came clean before things got even more out of control.

After her text, Molly dropped her phone on the side table and rolled over. Her mind played with Phelix's parting words. How was he going to come back to check on her later? The apartment doors automatically locked when it shut. Had Mandy given Phelix a key to her apartment? She worried about him coming over and trying his key in her door to find out it didn't work, or worse, going into Mandy's apartment and finding out her sister wasn't sick. How much of a problem was this going to cause? Molly pushed the worries away and wiggled deeper into her covers to sleep. She would worry about those things later.

Ten

"HOW ARE YOU FEELING?" MANDY ASKED AS SHE BRUSHED the hair back from her sister's face. Her twin did not look good at all.

"Sick," Molly grumbled as she clutched the blanket closer to her. "Cold."

Mandy watched as her sister shivered under her blankets. She held a thermometer out to check her sister's temperature.

Molly took the plastic covered probe and held it under her tongue.

"I'm so sorry," Mandy apologized as she watched the numbers climb. "I bet you caught this from me."

Molly grunted around the thermometer, but didn't really say anything.

As soon as the thermometer beeped, Mandy pulled it out and looked at the numbers. They were much higher than they should be, but not high enough to be alarming.

"But, Phelix brought me home today," Molly said.

Mandy stared at her sister as her twin's words sank in. "He did *what?*" she asked hoping that she hadn't heard her sister correctly.

"Phelix brought me home," Molly said again. "He'd stopped by for lunch again today."

Fury made Mandy draw in a slow breath. *Phelix broke his word again!* Trying to keep her rage in check, she let the air out as calmly as she could. Her sister was not the one that deserved the sharp side of her tongue. "What happened?" she asked when she was sure she wouldn't yell. She closed her eyes and listened to her sister's story.

"He was waiting out in front of the building when I came down," Molly explained. "I couldn't make it through lunch, so he took me back and told my boss he was taking me home."

Mandy blinked a few times in disbelief. "Wait," she interrupted, "he told Mr. Baker he was taking you home and that jerk didn't have anything snotty to say?"

Molly shook her head. "No," she said "I don't know why, but I think he recognized him. Called him Fair-something."

"Fairlane," Mandy said, confirming Phelix's last name. She paused and thought about it. "But, why would your boss know my boyfriend?"

"Phelix did say he knew one of the doctors in the building," Molly answered. "Maybe he's run into Mr. Baker before."

The idea that Phelix had run into Mr. Baker at Molly's work seemed plausible to Mandy, especially if Phelix had a friend in the building. She made a mental note to ask him about it later. "Point," she said before turning her consideration to her sister's flushed completion. She did genuinely look sick. Maybe Mr. Baker decided that it was better to let Molly go home versus having her be sick at work. "What else happened?"

"Not much," Molly said. "He called a cab and brought me home," she explained. "Although I am concerned with the fact that he brought me to my apartment instead of yours."

"He hasn't been in my apartment," she admitted. The fact that Phelix had been in Mandy's place so many times irritated Molly. When all of this was over, she would need to find a realistic reason to have moved apartments. Several possible excuses passed through her mind, but she pushed them away for now and finished explaining things to her sister. "He usually picks me up out front. And his place is better." He had a really nice house with lots of space. It made more sense to hang out there than it did in her small apartment.

"Really?" Molly asked. There was a surprised

lilt to her voice that made Mandy blush.

"He's got a really nice house," she admitted. "What else?"

"Well, um… he forced some pills and water on me and then…" she paused and scrunched up her face in remorse. "I kind of yacked them up."

"*Eewwww!*" Mandy squealed. She squirmed at the thought of her sister puking in front of her boyfriend. "Please tell me you did *not* make him clean that up." She looked around for possible signs of wayward yack.

The color on Molly's cheeks deepened. "No," she said softly. "I made it to the bathroom." She grimaced as she went on. "But he did hold my hair back."

"Molly!" Mandy sighed indignantly.

"What was I supposed to do?" Molly cried. "It's not like I chose to get sick or to have your boyfriend take care of me."

Mandy sat up away from her sister, surprised by the sudden outburst of tears.

"I didn't *want* any of this!" Molly sobbed. "I never *asked* to go on a date with your boyfriend! I didn't *want* to have sex with him! I never *asked* for him to show up at work and take me out to lunch! I've done everything I could think of short of being cold to him to get him to stop! It's not my fault that he is kind and considerate and cares about you! You should be *happy* that he's willing to take care of you while you're sick!" Molly clenched her jaw shut as the color drained from her face. Her hand jumped up to her mouth as she burped. Throwing back the covers, she bolted toward the bathroom.

Biting her lip, Mandy followed her twin and stood in the doorway as her sister curled on the floor, retching up bile. She felt horrible for dragging her sister into this situation. "I'm sorry, Molly," she apologized as she came into the bathroom. Picking up a hand towel from the edge of the sink, she ran some water over one end and handed it down to her sister. "I will see what I can do about Phelix." She was going to have to find a way to make her boyfriend keep his promise. This whole sordid affair was starting to put a strain on her sister. If she didn't do something soon, that stress was going to bleed over into their relationship.

Taking the towel, Molly wiped her face and hands before resting her head on the side of the bathtub. "Thanks," she said. "But we have a more pressing issue."

Mandy swallowed as she waited for her sister to continue. She met Molly's gaze and knew she was not going to like what her twin was going to say.

"Phelix is coming over this evening to check

on me," Molly warned. "Did you give him a key to your apartment?"

A mix of emotion raced down Mandy's back freezing her in place. Jealousy, anger, and fear warred for the top spot. When she could speak without screaming, she answered her sister's question. "No. Why?"

"Because I don't know how he's going to get back in," Molly said and closed her eyes. "See if you can find my keys."

Fear won out and Mandy quickly left to look for her sister's keys. They would most likely be in Molly's bag. Mandy hurried to the couch and rummaged through it looking for the keys. "They're not here," she called as she searched around any open surfaces where they might have been left. She hurried back to the bathroom.

Molly reached up for one of the bath towels and yanked it from the rack. "Then you'd better get out of here," she said. "I suspect he'll be back very soon." Tugging the towel over her, she held it tight as she stared up at her sister with a hopeful gaze. "Unless you would like to explain things to him."

Mandy licked her lips as she weighed her choices. She hated the idea of leaving her sick sister to the loving care of her boyfriend. Not only was it rude to abandon her twin, Mandy didn't like the idea of leaving them alone together. Phelix was everything she ever wanted in a man, and she didn't want to lose him to her sister. But, then again, he thought she and Molly were the same person.

"I'm not going to do anything," Molly huffed. "And if he tries something, I'll just puke on him."

Her sister's snarky attitude made Mandy smile in spite of the circumstance. "All right," she said as she turned to go. "I'm sorry, Molly."

"Oh, Mandy!" Molly called to her sister.

Stopping, Mandy held on to the frame of the bathroom door as she leaned back to see what her sister wanted.

"Get anything you wouldn't eat out of the refrigerator, just in case."

The thought of Phelix finding meat in Molly's fridge horrified Mandy. "Of course," she said as she stepped back into motion. Heading to the kitchen, she pulled open the refrigerator and stared at the contents. There was meat in practically everything. Pulling the trashcan close, Mandy opened up the first container ready to dump it out.

"And don't throw it away. I want it back when this is over!" Molly yelled from the bathroom.

Mandy's shoulders fell as she let out an aggravated sigh. Popping the lid back on the container, she set it back in the fridge and shut the door so she could find something to put everything in. She was going to have to hurry if she had any hope of cleaning out her sister's fridge and getting out of there before Phelix came.

"WHAT ARE YOU DOING?"

Molly looked up to find Phelix standing in the doorway. She swallowed back the vile taste in her mouth and licked her lips trying to get her voice to work. She had thrown up twice more since her sister had left her curled on the bathroom floor under a towel. "Throwing up," Molly confessed. "I figured it was easier to stay here than race back and forth from the bedroom."

Phelix let out a sigh and came to help her from the floor. "You're going to catch your death like this," he said as he helped her up from the cold tile floor. Once she was standing, he swept her from her feet.

Molly wrapped her arms around his neck and leaned into his hold. She smiled as his fingers plucked at the elastic strap holding her stockings up.

"What's this?" he asked in a teasing tone as he carried her from the room.

The smile on Molly's face grew. Raising one shoulder, she shrugged but didn't explain.

Phelix chuckled, sat her on the bed and unhooked the guarder belt from her waist. "Do you always wear thigh high stockings?" he asked, as he stripped the silky material from her legs.

"Sometimes" she lied. In truth, she almost always wore them, but her sister found the straps and belts uncomfortable.

"I see," Phelix said as he rolled them up and sat them on the table next to her bed. "Is there anything else that I should know about you?" he asked, raising a curious eyebrow.

Molly chewed on her lip and considered telling him that she was his girlfriend's twin, but she didn't think Mandy would appreciate that. Instead, she just shook her head. When Phelix's look turned pointed, she was sure he knew something was up, but he didn't push the subject. She sighed in relief when he let the issue go and pulled the blankets over her.

"Then rest here and I'll see about dinner."

Just the thought of food made Molly's stomach churn. She shook her head and rolled away from him hoping he would get the hint.

The sound of soft chuckling filled the air as Phelix patted the blanket over her. "Get some rest." Heading out of the room, he pulled on the door so only a crack of light shone in from the hall.

Pulling her phone from under her pillow, she swiped the screen open and looked at her missed messaged.

He's here!

She snickered softly as she considered the warning from her sister. Clicking the chat box open she sent her sister a note. *Figured that out. He found me on the bathroom floor. Did you get the meat out of the frig?*

Of course. What you doing on floor?

Trying not to throw up?

LOL. You should be in bed.

There now. He made me go back.

AWWW. So sweet.

Should I tell him you think so? Molly grinned as she sent this one.

NO!! No telling him.

Molly giggled.

"What's funny?"

Molly dropped her phone face-down on the comforter and looked up to find Phelix coming in with a tray of dishes. "Nothing," she said a little too fast.

Phelix's eyes narrowed, but he didn't call her out on the lie

The untruth didn't sit well, so she picked the

phone up and looked at the message once again trying to decide what was safe to tell him. "One of my friends was checking to make sure I was okay," she explained. "I told her someone was here taking care of me, and she was giving me a hard time." She turned off the screen and laid it back on the bed before meeting his gaze. The amused look on his face lightened her heart. She hated lying to him.

"That was sweet of them." He set the tray on the bed over her. "Here."

Molly considered the little, wooden tray and the mug of orange stuff it held. "I'm not really hungry," she admitted.

Phelix lifted the mug up and pressed it into her hands. "I know, beautiful, but you really should try to eat something."

Giving in, she closed her hand around the warm mug and brought it closer. "What's this?" she asked looking at the odd liquid.

"Jell-O."

Molly shot him the same disbelieving look he'd given her earlier. "This is not Jell-O," she said, swirling the stuff in the cup around.

"It's warm Jell-O," Phelix amended. "It doesn't look all that great, but I promise that it will help."

Drawing in a deep breath, Molly let it rush out before raising the glass to take a tentative sip.

The heat from the liquid carried the fruity scent of oranges up into her head while the juice rolled across her tongue and coated her mouth. She licked her lips as she stared down at the appeasing food. "And this is good for me?" She took another careful sip of the liquid.

"It has the sugars you need to function, water to help keep you hydrated, and it's easy on the stomach," Phelix explained as he sat on the edge of the bed near her feet. "Just don't drink it too fast, or you'll be back in the bathroom throwing up again."

Molly nodded. "Where did you learn all of this stuff?"

This time Phelix was the one that shrugged off her question. "You learn a lot of interesting things when there's a doctor in the family," he admitted. "He has a tendency to over share the grossest things at dinner so he can get the tastiest bits from the table."

She tried not to laugh around the mouthful of liquid she'd just taken, but only succeeded in sucking some down the wrong way. The coughing fit that followed made him jump up and take her cup away before she could slosh it everywhere.

"I'm sorry," he said as he rubbed her back.

She glanced up to find an amused, yet pained expression on his face. "That was so wrong," she said when the coughing fit finally subsided.

Phelix grinned as he set the cup on the side table. "True," he said, "but it made you laugh."

Molly chuckled again. "True," she agreed. Clearing her throat, she leaned back against her pillows. "But I think it upset my stomach again."

Phelix placed his hand on her head and checked her temperature. "You're still running a fever," he said. "Why don't you get back under those covers, and try to get some more rest? You can finish this later." Picking up the small table, Phelix lifted the blanket up so Molly could slide back into bed properly.

Molly glanced at the cup of cooling liquid. "But what if it sets up?"

Phelix kissed the side of her head. "Then I'll bring you a spoon. Now, get some rest." He tucked the wooden tray up under his arm and turned to go.

"Hey," Molly called after.

He turned back and raised an eyebrow in question.

"How did you get back into my apartment?"

A sheepish smile slipped across his face. "I borrowed your keys." Turning around, he left, leaving the door ajar just a crack.

Chuckling again, Molly rolled over in the bed and pulled out her phone. *Your bf is devious.* She typed to her sister.

Her sister's response was quick. *How so?*

He stole my keys to get back in and try to kill me with warm Jell-O.

Warm Jell-O?

He gave me warm Jell-O *for my upset stomach. Said it was good for me.*

There was a pause before her sister responded. *Don't eat it... not vegan.*

What?

Gelatin is made from animal proteins. Don't eat it.

Too late. You will just have to suck it up, buttercup. Molly grinned. She knew this was going to annoy her sister. The response that came back made her chuckle.

Grrrrr.

LOL.

There was another pause before Mandy answered. *Can I come up, or is he staying?*

Molly listened closely and could hear Phelix mucking about in her house. *I think he's staying. I can hear him in the kitchen.*

**SIGH* Okay, let me know what happens.*

I will. Going back to sleep for a while.

Get better.

Molly closed out of the messages from her sister and noticed that she had one message from a number she didn't know. She clicked it open and smiled at the text.

Hey, Beautiful. Just texting to let you know that I'm on my way. I hope you're doing okay. See you soon.

Reading through the message a second time, Molly snuggled down into her blankets with her phone. It made her happy that he had sent her the message. She closed her eyes, and drifted back off to sleep holding her phone. It didn't even occur to her that he hadn't sent the message to her sister's phone.

Eleven

MOLLY STOOD IN THE HALLWAY AND STARED AT THE MAN asleep on her couch. She licked her dry lips, and tried to sort out the ball of emotion rolling around inside her. Joy and sadness warred for the top spot as she watched Phelix sleep. Finding that he'd stayed touched her heart, but her feelings were soured by the truth of the matter. He was only there because he thought she was her sister.

Biting back her bitterness, she forced herself to push her emotions away and pulled out her phone. Snapping a quick picture, she sent it off to her sister. Molly told herself that she was doing it to show Mandy how much Phelix cared, but, deep inside, she knew it would annoy the hell out of her twin. Just a little payback for all the heartache she was feeling over the situation.

Turning away from the endearing sight, Molly made her way to the kitchen to find something to quench the thirst that had woken her. She hoped some cool water would ease some of the irritation bubbling inside her.

The light from the window lit the room just enough for Molly to find the sink. Flipping open the tap, she rinsed out a glass and sat it on the counter. She reached for the refrigerator, and pulled open the door. The sight that met her made her sigh. All of the food was gone. Mandy had been very thorough in cleaning out her well-stocked fridge.

Molly paused, surprised to find there was still something left. Reaching out she picked up a container she didn't recognize and popped the top off. The smell of tomatoes wafted up and she stared at the sauce covered noodles. There were chunks in the tub that looked like bits of hamburger. Definitely something her sister would not have left in the refrigerator.

Glancing around, Molly checked to make sure no one was watching before dipping the tip of her pinky in the sauce. Slipping the digit into her mouth, she sucked the savory sauce from her finger. It was amazing. Licking her lips, she popped the top on what could only be Phelix's lunch. She put the first container back and pulled out the second. This one contained some kind of puddingish stuff. She considered sampling this dish, but decided better. Popping the top back on the container, she put it back and pulled out the water filter.

Shutting the door, she screeched and nearly dropped the pitcher. Phelix was leaning against the wall behind the door. "Don't do that," Molly said as she grabbed her chest and turned to set the pitcher on the counter top. She gripped the edge of the counter and drew in several deep breaths, trying to calm her racing heart.

Stepping away from the wall, Phelix came into the kitchen. "I'm sorry," he said as he drew her into his arms and rubbed her back soothingly. "What are you doing out of bed?"

Molly tensed as his arms wrapped around her. She felt bad for letting him comfort her, but she didn't dare tell him the truth. Here sister would kill her. Letting out a sigh she let the warmth of his arms drain away the tension. "I was thirsty."

Phelix tilted his head over and rested his cheek on top of her head. "You could have called," he said softly. "I would have brought you something."

A soft noise born in contentment slipped from her as she leaned into him. "I didn't know that you were here," she admitted, enjoying the way his hands caressed the muscles of her back. "I didn't think you would stay." His soft laughter rumbled through her.

"Of course I stayed," he said. "I wouldn't leave

you alone while you're sick." He cupped the back of Molly's neck. "It seems you're still running a low-grade fever." Releasing her, he stepped back and reached for the water jug. He picked up Molly's glass and poured her some water, then handed her the tumbler. "Here." Turning around, he put the pitcher back in the refrigerator, and picked her phone up from the counter top. "Let's get you back to bed." Wrapping his arm around her, Phelix pressed his hand into her lower back and encouraged her to move.

Molly's heart fluttered as he escorted her back to bed. Turning her head, she stole a quick glance at the couch as they passed. It was a comfy couch to relax on, but she didn't like sleeping on. "Are you comfortable on the couch?"

Phelix shrugged. "It's a nice couch."

A smile stole across Molly's face. She loved the way he avoided answering her question. An idea struck, and she bit her lip unsure if the idea was good. She peeked at the dark shirt and pajama pants Phelix wore and hardened her resolve as they entered her bedroom. When they reached the edge of her bed, Molly turned around, took a deep breath, and looked up at her sister's boyfriend. "If you'd like, you could join me," she offered. Heat rushed across her cheeks and she glanced away, embarrassed that she'd made the offer.

Phelix closed the small space between them, and pulled her into his embrace once again. "I would like that," he said softly into her hair.

Molly's heart jumped at his acceptance.

Dropping his arms, he stepped back. "But only to sleep," he said as he circled the end of the bed to the other side. "I have an early day tomorrow, and you still need to rest and recover."

Chuckling to herself, Molly slipped back into bed and pulled her covers over her. She wiggled into place, hugging the edge of the bed. She felt the bed behind her dip down under Phelix's weight. "Good night," she called over her shoulder.

"Good night, beautiful," Phelix replied.

Molly tried to relax as she waited for Phelix to settle into the bedding. She'd expected him to stay on his side of the bed, but was surprised when his warm hand touched her back. Rolling toward him, she turned to see what he wanted.

"Come here," he said as he pulled her toward him.

"No," Molly protested. "I'll get you sick."

Phelix shushed her as he tucked her in against his body. "I'm probably going to get sick anyway," he admitted. "It doesn't take much to pass on a stomach bug."

Molly tensed in his arms as she thought about that. Mandy was going to be royally pissed if Phelix came down with this stomach flu.

"Relax," Phelix said as he ran his hand down her back. "It will be fine."

Letting out a deep sigh, Molly relaxed in his arm.

"Now go to sleep."

Nodding once more, Molly let the tension drain from her body, and savored the way she and Phelix fit together. It was heavenly. Hopefully, her sister would forgive her just this once. After all, she was sick. Molly fell asleep to the feel of Phelix's fingers rubbing soft circles into her skin.

THE SOFT LIGHT LEAKING AROUND THE CURTAINS WOKE Molly from her slumber. Drawing in a deep breath, she stretched the sleep from her limbs and relaxed back. She laid there taking stock of her situation. The queasiness in her stomach was gone, but she still had a slight ache behind her eyes.

Rolling away from the window, she looked over at the far side of the bed. The dent in the pillows and rumpled sheet showed where Phelix had been, but he was long gone. Molly sighed as she thought about her night. Although she'd enjoyed falling asleep in his arms, she shouldn't have invited him to bed. Her sister was going to be furious when she found out.

After giving herself a mental scolding, she turned over to get out of bed. Light from the window shone through the glass of water, and sent rays of color dancing across a folded piece of paper propped up on the table. Molly picked it up and read the scrawling handwriting. There was something oddly familiar about the way he made his letters. She was sure she'd seen those same curly characters on something other than his notes, but she couldn't remember where.

Good morning, Beautiful. I left some breakfast in the fridge for you. There are also some pills on the counter in the kitchen. Please take them. You still had a fever when I left so rest easy today. I'll speak with your boss to let him know that you won't be in, so please don't worry about it. Call me if you need anything. XXX

Molly didn't need a signature to know who had left the note. A smile curled her lips and she slipped the paper in the drawer with the last note Phelix had left. Usually, she was a light sleeper, but twice now he had gotten up from her bed without waking her. She shook her head, and picked her phone up from the table next to the water. Swiping the screen to life, she looked at the first message that popped up

Are you alive?

Her smile widened as she read over the message her sister sent at six am. She rolled down to the next message her twin sent.

Seriously, text me as soon as you wake up. The time stamp on the second message was seven thirty.

Molly chewed on her lip as she considered what to say to her sister. Another envelope icon flashed at the top of the screen, catching her attention. Closing out of her sister's messages, she tapped into the new text.

Hey, Beautiful. It's lunch time and I couldn't help thinking about you. It's lonely here without you. I hope you are getting some good rest. I'll stop by after work.

Molly looked at the time stamp on this text and found that it had only been a few minutes since it arrived. *Hey there. Just woke up*. She tapped out hoping Phelix hadn't gotten back to work yet. She'd just finished sending the same message to her sister when a reply from Phelix popped back up on the screen.

How are you feeling, Beautiful?

Molly wiggled in her seat happy that he had responded so quickly. *Like something the cat dragged in.*

LOL. Figured as much. There are meds on the counter. Take them if you haven't. They will help you sleep.

Molly laughed. *Trying to knock me out?*

You need sleep to recover properly. Besides, how else am I supposed to take advantage of you if you're still awake when I get back?

A blush raced over Molly's cheek and she tapped out her reply. *So bad! Did you steal my keys again?*

:) *How else am I supposed to get back in?*

Knock like a normal person.

Where's the fun in that? Besides, this way I can come and go as I please. A second message popped up before Molly could respond. *Hmm, maybe I should make a copy of this key.*

Molly giggled at the tease. She didn't think he would actually make copies of her keys. Mandy wouldn't date someone that creepy. *Maybe I should get the locks changed.* She teased back.

: (Would you?

A heartfelt smile cooled her mirth. It touched her that Phelix was worried about her rejecting him. *No. I enjoy your company.*

Good, I enjoy your company too.

Molly's heart fluttered as she read over his message. She stared at his words trying not to let the bitter reality of her situation take away from the joy his feelings gave her. Before she could come up with a response, another message flashed across her screen.

Hey, I have to get back to work. I'll see you later, Beautiful.

Have a good day. She sent back.

Taking a moment, Molly closed her eyes and relaxed back to lie across her bed. She hadn't realized how happy hearing from Phelix made her. Lifting her phone, she looked at the short exchange with Phelix again and sighed. Her sister was going to be pissed. Molly stared up at her ceiling and thought about what she was going to do about her growing feelings.

Her attention was pulled away from her problems when her phone pinged again. Raising it up, she read over the message from her twin.

Hey, sis! How you doing?

Pushing back her worries, Molly punched in a quick reply. *Better. Still have a headache.*

Not good. BTW loved the picture. He's so cute.

Molly was glad that her sister didn't seem upset by the situation. *I was surprised to find him on the couch. Thought he would have left.*

Kind of figured he would stay.

Molly raised an eyebrow at her sister's message. She wondered if her sister had come to that conclusion before she'd left Molly on the bathroom floor. Letting it go, Molly tapped out another message. *He really does love you.* It hurt to admit it, but it was obvious that the man was head of heels for her sister.

I know. He texted me to see how I was doing.

That statement bothered Molly. She read over her sister's words again not sure she understood them properly. Why was Phelix texting Mandy when he'd just been texting her? Curiosity made her bite the tip of her tongue as she sent her next text. *What did he say?*

Not much, just to take it easy and get better.

That still boggled Molly's mind. Why was Phelix sending texts to two different numbers? Trying to figure it out only made her aching head hurt more, so she let it go. There had to be a rational explanation, but she couldn't think of it at the moment. A soft growl from her stomach drove the issue out of her mind. *Going to go find food.*

Take it easy. I will stop by after work.

Molly closed out of her messages, picked up her water, and headed to the bathroom to brush her teeth. She had a desperate need to get rid of the foul taste in her mouth before finding food.

With freshly brushed teeth and a washed face, Molly made her way out to the kitchen. True to his word, Phelix had left a dish with three little pills and a note reading *take them all*. Smiling, she picked up the pills and chased them down with the water. Since her stomach was feeling better, opened the fridge to see what Phelix had left her.

Molly laughed as she pulled out a bottle of orange sports drink and a covered bowl. The little sticker on them made her feel like Alice. One simply said *Eat Me* while the other said *Drink Me*. She set the pair on the counter and took a picture. Adding the tagline, *Some Bunny left me a snack,* she shot the picture off to her sister.

The line of question marks her sister sent back made Molly snort. She knew her sister really wasn't the bookish type, but Molly had been sure her twin would recognize the reference to Lewis Carroll's most celebrated work. *You're hopeless,* she sent back with a quick explanation. Dropping her phone on the counter, Molly turned her attention to the container Phelix had left. The bowl was filled with a thick porridge-like substance. She wrinkled her nose at the white mass and took a picture of the goop.

What is this? She attached the message to the picture and sent it off to Phelix.

Molly sent the picture to her sister. *Your boyfriend is trying to poison me.*

The message from Mandy popped back within seconds. *What is that?*

Staring at the thick substance, Molly speculated on what it could be. *Wallpaper paste?* She joked. Molly tapped the surface of the food. It was soft and slightly tacky. She licked the residue from her finger and found that it was starchy with a hint of apple. *Tasty wallpaper paste!* She sent to her sister.

Another message flashed on her screen and she switched away from the conversation with her sister to what Phelix had to say.

I see you found lunch.

What is it? Molly typed back.

Rice porridge with apple juice for flavor. You can heat it up if you like.

Molly looked at the bowl and considered the meal. It would definitely taste better warm. *Thanks.* Setting her phone on the counter, she took the bowl over to the microwave to zap it. A few minutes should be more than enough to take the chill off the food. Once the food was warm, Molly collected the bowl and took it out to the couch where she could relax and enjoy her meager lunch.

twelve

"Hey there, Beautiful."

Molly woke up to Phelix's soft touch on her cheek. She drew in a deep breath and pushed back the blanket she'd found on her couch.

"What are you doing out here?"

Her eyes focused on the man standing over her and she blinked several times trying to make sense of what was going on. The drugs she'd taken muddled her mind, but she quickly recognized her visitor. "What time is it?" she mumbled. Scrubbing her knuckle into her eye, she sat up and looked around at her darkened living room. She didn't remember falling asleep.

"Just past five," Phelix said.

Molly's mind whirled around in surprise as she watched Phelix slip out of his jacket and start yanking on his tie. She couldn't believe that the day had slipped by so quickly. Something tickled at the back of her mind. She had a feeling that she was forgetting something important, but the more she grasped at it, the further it slid from her mind.

"So did you like lunch?" Phelix asked, pulling Molly's mind away from whatever she was trying to remember.

She looked up at him and smiled. "I really liked the labels," she said, pointing to the slips of tape on the table. "Made me feel like I was in Wonderland."

Gathering up the dishes, Phelix carried them to the kitchen as he answered. "I'm glad you caught the reference."

"Twas brillig, and the slithy toves did gyre and gimble in the wabe: All mimsy were the borogoves, and the mome raths outgrabe," Molly rambled out the first lines of poetry. Phelix warm laugh echoed out of the kitchen with the sound of running water.

"The *Jabberwocky* from *Through the Looking-Glass*," he called, identifying the passage. Stepping out of the kitchen, he met Molly's gaze. "Well read, and beautiful," he said. "What else should I know about you?" His crystal blue eyes flashed making Molly's breath catch.

Heat rushed over her face as her skin reddened. She licked her lips trying to decide if she should tell him the truth. She and her sister were very different in the types of things they liked and knew.

When they were younger, Molly had spent her free time pouring through any book she could get her hands on, while her sister had gone to the more social side of life. If things continued like this for much longer, Phelix was going to find out about their lie.

Drawing in a breath, she opened her mouth to tell Phelix the truth, but was distracted when her phone pinged. Molly picked it up and stared at the note from her sister. That nagging feeling at the back of her mind slammed into place, and she remembered what she had forgotten.

"I have to get the mail!" Molly squeaked and popped up from the couch. Clutching the blanket around her, she rushed to the door and ripped it open before Phelix could say anything.

REACHING OUT TO KNOCK ON HER SISTER'S DOOR, MANDY was shocked when the thing flew open. "Molly!" she cried in surprise.

Holding a blanket with one hand, Molly slammed the door behind her and grabbed Mandy by the arm spinning her around. "Move," she hissed.

Unsure what game her sister was playing, Mandy turned and followed her sister's pull as Molly dragged her across the landing and down the first flight of steps.

"Mandy?" Phelix's voice echoed through the hall above them.

Mandy's eyes widened in shock and she stared at her sister. Putting some extra pep in her step, she hurried down the rest of the steps and into her apartment before Phelix could catch them. They both leaned against the closed door and listened as Phelix came down the stairs looking for Molly.

"What's he doing here already?" Mandy whispered as she looked out the peephole. Phelix was just turning the corner to go down the stairs.

"He must have skipped out of work early," Molly said

Mandy turned around and glared at her sister. "Why didn't you tell me?"

Molly clutched the blanket around her tighter and huffed. "Give me a break," she snapped and went to sit on the couch. "I'm still groggy from the meds he gave me this afternoon."

Shock stole Mandy's anger. "He stopped by this afternoon?" she asked as her arms fell to her side. The thought of Phelix giving up his lunch to come take care of Molly stung.

"No," Molly said as she held the blanket around her. "He left some pills on the counter and instructions for me to take them when I woke up."

Molly's answer eased the pain in Mandy's heart. She turned around and peeked out the hole in the door as she tried to sort her feelings out. Her base emotions were hurt that her boyfriend was spending so much time with her sister, but the logical part of her brain told her she shouldn't blame her sister for the situation. Everything that was happening all lead back to her request for Molly to take her place at dinner.

Mandy watched as Phelix passed the landing and started back up the steps. "He's going back upstairs," she said as she turned around to face her sister. Phelix had not looked happy when he passed. "Where did you tell him you were going?"

"To get the mail," Molly answered.

Mandy stared at her sister. There was no way Molly was going to be able to get her mail as she was. The box took a key and it was clear to see that she did not have her keys with her. "The mail?"

Her twin gave her a pained look. "I'm sorry," she said. "I couldn't think of anything else. Your text said you were on your way up and I didn't want you just walking in."

Mandy froze and thought about that. Walking in on Molly and Phelix together would have exposed everything they were working to hide. "Right," Mandy said as she tried to figure out what to do. She didn't really want to leave her sister and her boyfriend together, but she didn't know how to keep them apart without explaining things to Phelix.

The tension and silence between the twins grew until Molly broke it. "So you want to switch clothing and go back up?" she offered.

Mandy stared at her sister, intrigued by the idea. How hard could it be to switch places with her twin and pretend to be sick? She took a calculating look at her twin's condition. Molly was in a wretched state. A woven blanket hung from her shoulders and barely covered the rumpled t-shirt she was wrapped in. Her hair hung limply around her shoulders with an oily sheen that showed it was in need of a wash.

Mandy crinkled her nose knowing she could never manage the look her sister had now. Not in the few minutes they had before Phelix started to worry. "I don't think so," Mandy said. She gave her sister a pained smile. "You look awful."

"Well, I have been sick," Molly grumbled.

"I know," Mandy said. "And I wish I could trade places with you, but I just can't manage this level of bad right now."

Molly snorted in amusement. "True," she admitted. "Besides, shouldn't you be leaving soon.?"

Thoughts of Mandy's trip ran through her head. She'd been planning this vacation for months, but she didn't want to leave her sister while she was ill. She bit her lip trying to decide what to do. "I can stay if you want me to."

Molly shook her head. "I'm doing much better," she admitted. "And I know how long you've been looking forward to this weekend. Besides, the problem isn't my health; it's your boyfriend." Desperation covered her face. "What am I going to do?"

Mandy could not think of anything that would help. Giving up her vacation wouldn't make Phelix leave while Molly was sick "I don't know."

"You need to tell him that we're not the same person," Molly pleaded. "Just come upstairs and tell him so we can get this over with."

Horror raced through Mandy as she thought about everything that would happen if she told Phelix the truth. She shook her head. "No," she insisted. She pinned her sister with a hard stare "And you're not going to tell him either. Just tell him you're feeling better and still want to go on the vacation. Get him out of there today and I will deal with him when I get back."

"He's going to find out," Molly whined.

"How? We are identical twins."

Molly glared at her. "Mandy, we're different enough that he is going to notice. He's not stupid."

Mandy let out a deep sigh and tried to reason

with her stubborn sister. "Look, just get through the weekend and I'll take care of this." Coming over, she sat on the couch next to her sister. "I promise." She gave her twin a hug. The irritated look on Molly's face spoke volumes to what her sister thought of her idea.

"What do you want me to do if he tries to get me in bed again?" Molly's voice was very pointed.

The thought of her sister sleeping with her boyfriend again irritated Mandy, but she didn't know what to tell her. Mandy let out a sigh, and hung her head. "Just get through the weekend, and I'll fix it on Monday." She looked up at her sister, unhappy with the situation. "Do your best to avoid anything."

Molly glared at her sister. "And if he came on to you, how would you push him away without hurting him?"

A sick feeling made Mandy's stomach roll. "I wouldn't," she admitted. "Just try your best." She looked up at the clock and tried to figure out how long it had been since her sister had left. "You need to get back upstairs before he really starts to worry."

"I really think you should tell him," Molly pushed once more.

Mandy stood up from the couch. "Not right now." She hoped she could find an answer that didn't involve telling him the truth. She just needed to find a way to stop Phelix from meeting up with Molly at lunch time. But, how was she going to convince him that lunch was a bad thing when he was just trying to make her happy.

Turning around, she helped her sister from the couch. "Just hang in there for the weekend and don't let him find out." Once her sister was stable, she went over to her TV stand and picked up her stack of mail. "Here," she said, handing the bundle to Molly.

Sighing, Molly took the envelopes and hugged her sister. "Have fun on your trip."

"Keep me updated," Mandy said. She opened the door and watched as her twin shuffled out. Closing the door, she turned back to look at her empty apartment and vowed to find a way to put an end to Phelix's lunch time visits, even if she had to spend her entire vacation plotting.

CLAMBERING BACK UP THE STEPS, MOLLY STOPPED IN FRONT of her door and stared at it. In her rush to get out, she'd forgotten to pick up the keys. Pulling in a deep breath, she let it rush from her and knocked on the door.

Phelix did not look happy when he opened

the door. "Where did you go?" he asked as he stood out of the way to let her in.

"To get the mail," Molly said as she held out the stack of letters her sister had given her.

Phelix took the stack of letters from her hand and looked at them. "And these couldn't have waited for you to get dressed?" he asked as he tossed the letters down on the coffee table. He glanced down at what Molly was wearing.

Molly let out another sigh. "I guess not."

Reaching out, Phelix wrapped his arms around her and pulled her closer. "Where did you go?" he asked again in an upset tone. "I tried to follow you out, but you disappeared."

Molly leaned into his warmth and tried to think of a plausible excuse. "To the manager's office," she lied. "I'm expecting a package that's too big for the mailbox, and I needed to check on it before the office closed." This wasn't exactly untrue. She had placed an order online for some books that weren't going to fit in her mailbox, but those weren't supposed to be in until next week.

"Well, don't run off like that again, beautiful." He hugged her harder against him. "It makes me worry."

Molly buried her face in his chest as he kissed her hair. "I'm sorry." She clutched his shirt as she tried to contain her emotions. His concern touched her, and made her want to cry out her frustration with the situation.

"It's okay," Phelix said as he ran his hands down her back. Leaning forward, he nuzzled the hair at the side of her neck. "You're wearing my blanket." He punctuated his words with a soft kiss to her neck.

Molly fidgeted in his arms. "I was cold."

Putting a little space between them, Phelix lifted his hand up to her cheek and raised her face to him. "Let me see if I can warm you up." He leaned in to capture her lips.

She pressed against his chest, and kept him from his goal. "I'm still sick," she protested.

Phelix let out a soft snort of amusement. "I don't care," he said as he molded her body to his and claimed her lips.

Curling her fingers into his shirt, Molly closed her eyes and melted into his kiss. The warm tip of his tongue traced across the seam of her lips, working to deepen their embrace. Letting him in, Molly released the hold she had on his shirt and wrapped her arms around his back. She held on as his mouth washed most of the world away. The only thing present in her mind was the feel of him pressing her against his front, and a hot ball of desire building deep inside her.

When they finally broke apart, they were both

panting in need. Molly kept her eyes closed and let her head loll back as he nibbled on her lower lip. Phelix kissed her lightly, drawing her back to him. She opened her gray eyes and stared into his crystal blue ones.

"Amazing," he whispered.

Molly was sure that she could see his soul deep in those dilated pupils. Shifting her gaze from one eye to the other, Molly could also see the desire riding him. A wave of consciousness washed over her and she stiffened in his arms. How could she be doing this to her sister?

Concern drove some of the passion from Phelix's eyes as she released her hold on him and tried to step out of his grasp. "What's wrong?"

The tip of Molly's tongue slipped over her lower lip as she tried to find some excuse for her action. Her body was screaming at her to continue, but the feelings she had for her sister were sending her on a major guilt trip. "I need a shower," she said as she pushed the rest of the way out of his arm.

Understanding drove the concern out of Phelix's eyes. "Of course," he said as he let her slip from his hold.

Stepping out of his reach, she dropped the blanket on the couch, grabbed her phone, and bolted to the bathroom. Shutting the door behind her, she leaned on it and slid down to the floor. She clicked open her phone and sent her sister a message. *You should cancel your trip this weekend.*

Mandy's response was quick. *What happened?*

He kissed me as soon as I got back into the apartment.

There was a short pause before a new message pinged back. *...and what did you do?*

Molly stared at her sister's question before responding. *I told him I needed a shower and ran off to the bathroom.*

Good move! But be careful. Phelix can be persistent.

Anger and fear raced up Molly's spine. *OMG! Come up here and tell him. I don't know if I can handle this.* She stared at her phone waiting for her sister's response, hoping it wasn't the same answer Mandy had already given her.

No. You can do this.

Molly clenched her teeth and glared at her phone. That was not the answer she was hoping for. Drawing her knees to her chest, she wrapped her arms around them and thought about how to respond to her sister. Frustration made her want to scream, but she didn't dare do anything to draw Phelix's attention. She stared at her sister's messages one more time, and tried to find a calm center in the desire and frustration swirling through her. She hated the situation her sister was putting her in, but she couldn't think of a way around it without destroying her sister's relationship. *Okay.* She typed out. *One more weekend, but you will fix this on Monday.*

Her sister's response was quick. *Yes. Promise.*

Thank you. Molly let out a sigh of relief and sent her sister one last message. *Going for a shower now. Have a good weekend. TTYL.* Punching the power button, she turned off her phone and dropped it on the floor behind the door. She dragged herself up from the floor, and leaned on the sink to stare into the mirror. What she saw horrified her.

She had no idea how Phelix could think her sickly complexion was beautiful. There were still traces of makeup clinging to the lower edges of her eyes, and her hair was a god-awful mess. She didn't remember someone trying to tame her blonde locks into a bundle at the back of her neck, but several bits had escaped and were clumped up in random tangles that would only come out with a good conditioning.

Wrinkling her nose in disgust, Molly turned away from the mirror and went to start her shower. She fiddled with the water until it was as hot as she could stand it before turning on the spray.

Stripping out of her clothing, she stepped into the hot water and drew the curtain closed. Her situation would look a lot better after she had a few minutes to relax and think things through.

The hot water splashed across Molly's body, relaxing the tension from her shoulders. Letting the water pound into her skin, she closed her eyes to process her predicament. What was she going to do about Phelix?

Her mind churned as she thought about what she would find when she got out of the shower. There was no doubt in her mind that he would still be out there waiting for her, ready to continue where they had left off. She toyed with the idea of staying in the shower all night, but pushed that thought away. It was quite likely that he would get worried after a while and come looking for her. Besides, the hot water wouldn't hold out that long. She'd have to come up with another excuse to avoid him.

Another notion popped into her head. She could tell him she was tired and just wanted to go to sleep. Rolling this idea over, Molly turned into the spray to let it hit her face. This plan held merit. She was just getting over being sick. He couldn't hold that against her. Reaching out, she rested her hands on the wall to lean under the faucet so the water could run over her head. The heat helped to break up the fuzz left by the medication. Now, she just had to find a way to relax her own emotions and desires away.

The ragged sigh Molly let out released most of the frustration she was feeling. Relaxing, she let the water wash her worries away, and allowed her mind to wander. It immediately rushed to the man in the other room, and how much she enjoyed the way he felt against her. Although she knew she shouldn't do it, she tilted her head further forward and let her imagination take her away.

She reveled in the sensation of the hot water pounding on her neck. It felt as if strong fingers were caressing her skin. Envisioning Phelix behind those fingers, she enjoyed her fantasy as those phantom hands slid to her shoulders and gently kneaded the tension from her muscles. Slowly, they worked their way down her shoulder blades. Molly let out a heavy sigh when they slid down to her sides soothing her cares away. Reality ripped through her fantasy as those imaginary hands gained substance and pulled her backward.

Molly gasped as her weight shifted back against a solid form. Turning her head, she found Phelix holding her from behind. "Phelix!" Molly cried out softly. She didn't understand how he had gotten there. She hadn't heard either the door or curtain open.

Phelix nuzzled her neck and kissed her damp skin. "Hey, beautiful." He squeezed her against him. "I came in to help wash your back."

Even from the odd angle, Molly could see the mischievous twinkle in his eyes. Now that the initial shock was starting to fade, Molly's mind split into two halves and screamed at her. One side told her that this was wrong and she needed to get him out of the shower, while the other side urged her to follow the desire burning between them and let things happen. She stiffened, not knowing which feelings to follow.

"Is everything okay, baby?" Phelix asked, as he moved so he could meet her eyes.

The concern in his voice pushed Molly to relax in his arms. Losing her cool would definitely give her secret away. She tried to think like her sister. Mandy would have loved for him to join her for a nice shower. "Yes," Molly said as she forced herself to relax, "you just surprised me." Closing her eyes, Molly leaned her head back so that it was resting against his shoulder. Raising her arms up, she settled them over his and tried not to let him notice the war raging inside her.

Phelix rubbed his cheek into her damp hair. "I hope it was a pleasant surprise."

Molly made a contented noise.

"Good," he said. His mouth found the side

of her neck, and drove the rest of the protesting voices out of Molly's head. She knew there would be hell to pay later, but the more he touched her, the less she cared about what her sister would have to say.

Pulling his mouth from her skin, Phelix breathed a suggestion in her ear. "Let's get you cleaned up."

The desire laced through his words lit a fire in Molly that she couldn't control. She giggled and squirmed in his arms. She followed the gentle push of his hands as he turned her around and placed her under the spray. The water drummed on her back, racing her pulse along.

"Let's start up here," he said, lifting his hands and running them over the top of Molly's wet hair, tilting her head back into the cascade of water.

Bending to his will, Molly closed her eyes and enjoyed the feel of his fingers massaging their way across her scalp. When the pressure let up, she opened her eyes and watched Phelix reach for the bottle of shampoo.

The smell of her peppermint shampoo tickled Molly's nose, and she grinned as Phelix worked a large amount into suds. She tried to keep her eyes from his bare skin, but the light shimmering off the water droplets drew her in. Her gaze followed the line of water trickling over his chest and down his stomach. Her eyes fell to the length at his groin and she quickly looked away. Knowing what he felt like and seeing him in his full glory were two different things. Anticipation and desire rolled through her, making her shiver in spite of hot water.

"Come here."

His soft command drew her attention to meet his passion filled eyes. The need to touch him coursed through her as she stepped out of the water. "Should I turn around?" Molly asked as she lacing her fingers together, trying to keep her hands to herself. Her chances of getting out of this weekend untouched had disappeared as soon as Phelix had decided to join her, but she still wanted to be able to tell her sister that she'd done her best to not encourage him.

Phelix grinned mischievously and closed the distance between them. "No. If you turn around, I can't do this." Wrapping his arms around her, he pulled her against his chest and slid his soap covered hands up the back of Molly's head.

She placed her hands on his chest for support and moaned as his fingers slipped up through her hair.

Weakened by the wonderful sensation, Molly slid her hands around to his back. She gripped him tightly and tilted her head back, giving him better access to the top of her head. Another sigh of pleasure slipped out as his fingers massaged the grime from her hair. The feel of his arousal pressing between their bodies made her insides quiver with excitement. Even if Mandy ripped open the curtain and screamed for them to stop, Molly knew that she wouldn't want to. There was something about this man that called to her, and she found that she could not deny it anymore.

Phelix's lips met hers as he smoothed her ruffled hair down. Thick suds dripped from her hair onto her shoulders and back. His fingers brushed the bubbles across her back as he kissed her.

Molly gasped as he pulled her in tighter.

Their initial kiss had been broken in her surprise, but he didn't stop. He laid hungry little kisses along her lips and jaw as his hands pulled a large cluster of suds over her shoulder. The bubbles dribbled down between them.

Molly grinned as Phelix shifted so the foam would slide between them. She raised an eyebrow at him. "Oh really?"

The left corner of his mouth turned up into a cockeyed grin as he pulled her against him again. "Oh yes," he whispered as he recaptured her lips. The soap squished between them while Phelix used his body to wash Molly's front side.

She moaned into his mouth as his hands slid

over the curve of her hip and cupped her right ass cheek. Closing her eyes, she stroked her fingers along his back encouragingly.

Running his hand down to her thigh, Phelix lifted her leg up to his hip. He pulled her up against him. His hard length was trapped between them, but it rubbed against her with just enough friction to make her shiver.

Molly opened her eyes when Phelix released her lips. She stared into his eyes as he held her.

"So beautiful," he sighed as he leaned back in to reclaim a kiss. Releasing Molly's leg, he leaned in, making her step back to retain her balance.

The spray of water bit at her body as he moved her farther under the faucet. The splash of the water over her shoulders forced him to end the exploration of her mouth. She drew in a much-needed breath as he pulled back. A growl rumbled up between them, and she could feel his irritation at having to give up his hold. She laughed as he guided her that final step into the water. Tilting her head back she let the water eat the soap from her body. She raised her hands and ran them through her hair.

The noise Phelix made was almost primal.

Molly opened her eyes just as he recaptured her, spun her around, and banged her into the wall.

She let out a squeak of surprise, but it did not last long under the demanding press of his lips.

Phelix's hands wandered Molly's body as his tongue explored her mouth. Cupping his hands to the cheeks of her ass, he leaned in, pressing her against the wall.

Molly let out another surprised cry as he jerked her up from the floor. Wrapping her arms around his neck, she held on for dear life as he pinned her to the wall. Somehow, Phelix managed to angle himself so his tip rubbed against her warm, wet folds. She moaned again as he found the spot he was looking for.

"May I?" he moaned into her mouth, holding himself back from actually entering her.

"Yes," she whispered back.

As soon as she'd breathed her permission, Phelix pushed into her, parting the skin.

She gasped as he filled her.

He paused part of the way in to allow her to adjust before easing himself out of her passage.

Molly let out a long moan as he pushed his length into her at an impossibly slow speed. Her body relaxed around him as he moved. "Oh, Phelix," she gasped.

He gave one final, hard thrust, driving a cry from her as he brought them together fully. He paused to let the sensation subside before he started in with more gentle movements.

Her breathing sped up as his motion drove her closer to a peak.

His mouth worked fervently at her neck as he found a solid rhythm. The soft gasps and moans escaping from Molly drove him on. He shifted his feet to get a better angle, and slipped in the water-slick tub. Throwing out a hand, Phelix caught himself on the small metal basket hanging from the shower head.

Crying out in surprise at the sudden instability, Molly clenched her legs and arms around him. Her inner muscles tightened around his swollen length making him groan.

Once they were stable again, he released his hold on the basket and gathered her back up in his arms. "We're going to kill ourselves doing this," he said, giving his hips a slight thrust to emphasize his words.

"Kill me," Molly moaned as the frictions drove the rest of the shock from her system.

Chuckling, he reached for the faucet and slammed the tap closed. "Hold on," he warned.

Molly clenched her legs around him, holding on tight.

The pressure drove another groan from him, and Phelix gave her one more good thrust before pushing away from the wall. He wrapped his arms around Molly's back and stepped out of the tub. Nudging open the door, he carried her out of the bathroom and down the short hall to the bedroom.

Grabbing the edge of the comforter, Phelix ripped the covers away exposing the sheets.

Molly giggled as he lifted his knee to the bed and leaned her back to the mattress still soaking wet.

"I love it when you do that," he rumbled as he pulled himself part of the way out of her.

Molly gave him a confused look. "Do what?"

"Giggle," Phelix answered, causing Molly to giggle again. His eyes rolled back as her muscles contracted around him. He moaned his enjoyment before recapturing her lips and finding the rhythm they had lost in the shower.

Molly's moans intensified as her pleasure grew. Her peak hit, and she cried out as she shattered in his hands.

Phelix slowed to match his strokes to the waves of her orgasm, while her nails bit into his skin as she convulsed. The extra bit of sensation pulled him into her pleasure, making him lose his concentration and burst inside her. Phelix gave one final thrust before collapsing on top of Molly, panting.

Gladly accepting his weight, Molly squeezed

him to her. Her fingers caressed his back as they lay together, enjoying the sensations seeping from their bodies.

"I'm so sorry," Phelix apologized as he pulled out and rolled to the bed next to her.

Molly looked at him confused. "For what?" she asked. She snuggled in his arms, not sure what he had to apologize for.

"I'm sorry," he said again. "I was planning on that lasting a lot longer, but nails..." A sheepish grin slipped across his face.

Molly giggled again. "Don't worry about it," she said before giving him a quick kiss. "Much more and I don't think I would have been able to move again tonight." As it were, she couldn't feel most of her body past the tingling of the fading orgasm.

Phelix laughed and cuddled her tighter. "I don't want you to move from me tonight."

A zing of ecstasy whipped through Molly, and she snuggled into him. She wanted to stay in this man's arms for as long as he would have her. Her emotions were dampened when thoughts of her sister pushed their way through her endorphin muddled mind. She relaxed in his hold, and tried not to let guilt eat her. A shiver ran up her back as the water evaporated from her skin and cooled her.

Phelix's warm hands rubbed over her cooling skin. "But I think we need to dry off before we both get sick."

Molly nodded her agreement. They rested together for a few minutes longer, not wanting to move from each other.

Finally, Phelix sighed and climbed off the bed. He turned back and held his hand out.

Molly let him help her from the bed and leaned against him as he wrapped his arms around and kissed her. After a few moments, he pulled back and held her while studying her face. Molly's breath caught as she saw something floating in his eyes. For a moment, she was sure that he knew she was lying to him. She bit her lip waiting for him to ask the question that would doom them all. After a heart-stopping moment, he let out a sigh and released her.

"Come on," he said, and took her by the hand again. "Let's go finish that shower and get dinner."

Molly drew in a relieved breath and followed him out. She was glad that he hadn't said anything. Her emotions were balanced on a point and if he'd pushed her at all, she would have spilled everything despite her sister's wishes.

Following Phelix's lead, she waited with her thoughts while he turned on the shower and climbed into the tub.

"Come here," he said as he pulled her over the edge and into the water once again. He leaned his back against the wall and guided her around so her back rested against his chest. The water poured over her, washing the traces of their sex from her body.

She relaxed into his chest and turned her face so the spray wouldn't drown her.

Phelix sighed into her hair and kissed her head. "Thank you," he said as he played with the water cascading over her torso.

Molly let out a contented sigh as he cupped his hands and caught the liquid running over her. When they were full, he shifted his fingers and let the water gush down her skin.

"I should be thanking you," she said, once she was sure her voice wouldn't show the guilt and agony eating at her. "You're the one who did all the work," she teased, trying to keep her darkening mood light. She tilted her head so she could look up at him.

"And it was oh so worth it," Phelix whispered in a husky voice. He craned his neck to find her lips, and kissed her for a moment before pulling back. Leaning his head back against the wall, he let out a deep sigh. "We need to get out of here or we'll never get dinner."

Molly chuckled, and stood up away from him.

Phelix's fingers trailed along her skin as she moved away.

"True," she said as she turned to rinse the tangles from her damp hair. "I am kind of hungry."

Letting out a soft growl, Phelix reached out and rubbed his hand down Molly's back. "I know what I'm hungry for."

His words and hungry look brought a bright blush to her skin.

"What?" Her voice squeaked from her, higher than usual.

A serious look crossed his face. Leaning in close, he let his finger trail across her skin. He breathed softly on her ear, sending chills of anticipation racing through her. "Stir fry," he whispered suggestively.

Molly's head snapped to look at the mischievous smile curled up the corner of his mouth.

He dropped a fast kiss on her lips, and patted her butt as he moved away from her. "Hurry up and finish while I get things started."

Molly just stared at him in shock as he got out of the shower.

"Take your time," he called as he yanked the plastic curtain closed between them.

Turning back to the water, Molly's mind raced as she picked up the bottle of conditioner. She squirted some in her hand and scrubbed it into her hair while trying to get her emotions under control. Phelix was special, but she had no rights to him. He was her sister's guy. She needed to find a way to crush the contented feeling he left in her.

THE BOWL OF RICE AND FRIED VEGETABLES THAT PHELIX SET on the table looked amazing.

"Thank you," Molly said as she scooted closer to the table. Unsure how to act around Phelix, she had taken her time in the shower so she could figure out what to do. She had carefully brushed and braided her damp hair, then gone to change the sheets on the bed while she searched for an answer. She had just finished tucking in the comforter when Phelix called her to dinner, but she still hadn't solved her problem. She still didn't know how to get Phelix to leave her alone, or if she really wanted him to.

"I hope you enjoy it."

Molly looked up to find Phelix watching her from the other side of the table. Picking up her fork, she poked it into the hot veggies. "Do you always cook like this?"

Phelix smiled. "Stir fry is the only vegan food I know how to cook," he admitted sheepishly.

"We'll have to change that," Molly said, and

dug into her meal. There were several recipes that she could teach him that were easy to make, meatless, and still very good. She shook her head to stop her brain from wandering to those possibilities. It wasn't good to daydream about spending more time with this man. He would be going back to her sister soon. Molly couldn't let herself get any more attached to him. "This is good," she admitted, trying not to look at the man across the table.

"Thank you," he replied. They ate on in a weird silence for a few minutes until Phelix cleared his throat and broke the awkward tension building between them. "Um… So, I talked with your boss and made sure that he wasn't expecting you in until Monday. Are you still planning on going on your trip this weekend?"

Molly looked up at him shocked. "What?"

"Your trip to the yoga thing, are you still going?" Phelix asked.

Molly sighed at her stupidity, how could she have forgotten her sister's yoga retreat. It only took a second for the idea to hit her, but suddenly Molly knew how she was going to save herself this weekend. "I don't see why I shouldn't," she said with a shrug. "I've been planning this for a while, and it's already paid for."

Phelix just stared at her with an oddly blank face.

Molly's heart pounded at his sudden stillness. There was a tightness around his mouth that made her think he was unhappy about something. "That is unless you don't want me to go." As soon as the words were out of her mouth, Molly wanted to smack herself for offering. If Phelix said he didn't want her to go, she would pretend to stay home. They would probably spend a wonderful weekend wrapped in each other's arms. That would be bad.

There would be no way she would be able to contain the guilt and feelings building inside her. It was inevitable that something would push her over the edge and she would admit everything to him. She fidgeted in her seat wanting him to say yes, but praying he would say no.

The hardness in his face melted into a smile, and he reached out to take her hand. "It really means a lot to me that you would consider my feelings," he said, rubbing her knuckles with his thumb. "But, since you've been planning this for such a long time, you should go."

The weight making her stomach churn lifted, and she smiled as disappointment settled into her heart. She hated losing the time with him, but she knew it was the right thing to do. "Thank you." It was hard to keep the disappointment from her voice. She squeezed his hand tightly before releasing it to go back to her meal.

Phelix picked up his fork and stirred his food around. "So when are you leaving?"

Molly sighed again and forced the pain she was causing herself away. She thought about the text she'd received from her sister saying she was leaving. It would take three hours for Mandy to get to the retreat. A real smile grew on Molly's face as she thought about how late it had already gotten. "It's too late to leave tonight," she said. "So I guess I'll head out in the morning."

His smile broadened. "Fantastic. That gives us a few more hours." His eyes turned heated as he leaned forward over his plate. "So what would you like to do after dinner?"

A light blush rose up Molly's cheeks as possibilities passed through her mind. Turning her attention to her food, she tried to hide her embarrassment. "I don't know," she said, stirring her rice around without meeting his gaze. "What would you like to do?" After what seemed like an eternity without an answering, Molly looked up at the grin curling his lips.

"I'm sure we can find something fun."

Molly's blush darkened at the suggestion in his voice. She swallowed hard as her pulse skipped in excitement. Whatever he had in mind, it wouldn't be good for her heart.

Thirteen

"Have a good weekend, and I'll see you on Monday," Phelix said, pausing in his prep to give Molly a hug.

She squeezed him back not wanting him to leave for work. They had spent most of the evening cuddled up on the couch watching a sci-fi marathon. Molly had laughed out loud when he had suggested the popular British time-traveling show. It had been one of her favorites growing up. "Take care." Stepping back from his arms, she pulled his blanket around her shoulders to hold out the chill of the morning air.

Phelix rubbed the blanket over her arms. "Send me a text, so I know that you got there safely." He leaned down to kiss her.

Molly caressed his chest through his thin, dress shirt. She liked the charcoal gray material of his suit. It made his eyes sparkle in an enticing way. "Of course," she agreed as they parted.

Standing up, he straightened his tie and turned to leave.

Concern flashed through Molly's mind as she realized he was going empty handed. "What about your stuff?" She looked over at his garment bag and pillow still sitting on her loveseat.

"I'll get it next week," he said as he reached out and stroked the backs of his fingers down the side of her face. "That is if it's okay with you?"

Pleasure bubbled through her as she leaned her head over into his touch. She loved the feel of his hands on her skin. "Sure," she agreed without thinking about it.

He rolled his fingers over to cup her cheek. "Then I will see you later." Raising her face to his, he kissed her one last time before slipping out the door.

Molly let out a contented sigh and leaned against the closed door. She savored the emotions coursing through her. Phelix made her happier than anyone she had ever known. Knowledge that she was in love with her sister's boyfriend dampened her mood, and she stepped away from the door. She would have to find a way to deal with her emotions before her sister got back.

Shaking her regret away, she glanced around the room trying to decide what to do now. Thanks to Phelix, she had the whole day to herself.

Going back to bed sounded like the best idea, and she headed to her room. Folding up the blanket around her, she dropped it on the foot of the bed before slipping between her sheets. She cuddled deep in the bedding, but couldn't get her mind to shut off. She and Phelix had spent another action packed night in her bed, and the cotton cloth still held their aroma. Molly hadn't noticed it when he was here, but now that he was gone, she could almost taste the spicy scent he'd left behind. Drawing in a deep breath, she savored the memories the smell brought back. It made the sore muscles in her belly pull and her heart long for him.

Throwing back the covers, Molly got out of bed. Being wrapped in those tantalizing sheets made her want for company she knew she couldn't have. Looking back at the bed, she considered changing the sheets. It was the best thing to do, but she just couldn't bring herself to do it. Mandy had promised to put an end to Phelix's lunch time visits when she got home, so last night might have been the last time she saw him. Pulling the covers up, Molly made the bed. These sheets were fresh when she put them on last night, and she would have to wash her other set before she could use them. Having his scent in her bed would not sway her into making more laundry than she already had.

Having taken care of the bed, Molly pulled a t-shirt and some sweatpants from the dresser. She loved the strappy black nightgown Phelix had picked out last night, but it was much too thin to wear for the day. She pulled it off, remembering how he had laughed when she put it back on this morning. It had, after all, spent most of the night on the floor. She draped it over the bed spread to deal with later.

Once dressed, Molly grabbed her phone and took Phelix's blanket to lie on the couch. She was still a little tired and didn't really want to do anything. After a quick text to her sister, she found a comfortable place to curl on one end of the couch. Closing her eyes, Molly let her mind wander back to the night before, and the time she had spent cuddled next to Phelix. She was really going to have to do something about the feeling swirling through her. A ding from her phone announced her sister's response.

Morning. How was your night?

Molly laughed and tapped in response. *Interesting… In the old Chinese proverb way.*

???

Molly was surprised her sister didn't catch the reference to the old Chinese curse: May you live in interesting times. Molly had used the saying around her sister many times. *I think I'm starting to really like your boyfriend.* She admitted.

There was a long pause before Mandy's response pinged through. *You're not supposed to start liking him.*

Irritation made Molly's fingers fly across her phone. *I know, but it's hard to not like someone after sleeping with them three times. Plus he is super nice and smart.* She sent the inflaming comment off before thinking about it.

THREE TIMES!!

The large print of her sister's message made Molly regret that she had snapped that message at her sister, but there was nothing she could do about it now except admit the truth. She blew out a breath as she explained. *Yes, three. You were right when you said he was persistent. He decided to join me in the shower, and then he followed me to bed.*

Molly!! How could you!

Clicking on her caps lock, Molly punched the message into her phone as hard as she could, pissed at the accusing tone of the message. *IT'S NOT LIKE I WAS GIVEN MUCH CHOICE IN THIS. HAD YOU TOLD HIM THE TRUTH THEN I COULD HAVE STOPPED IT FROM HAPPENING!* It was a few minutes before Mandy responded again.

I'm sorry. I'll talk to him when I get back on Sunday night.

Are you going to tell him the truth, or just get him to stop coming by at lunch? Molly bit her lip, praying that her sister would agree to tell Phelix the truth.

Can we talk about this later? I have to get to yoga.

Molly growled at her sister's answer, but didn't see a reason to continue this fight through text. *Fine, but you need to tell him the truth. He deserves to know.* She prayed her sister would heed her warning.

Mandy didn't respond to this message.

Irritated with the way the conversation had ended, Molly tossed her phone down on the coffee table. Getting her sister to admit to the lie would take an act of Congress, but Molly also knew that admitting the truth had the potential to cause her sister some very real problems. They had both told a lie big enough to end Mandy's relationship.

Molly draped her arm over her eyes and sighed as she thought about the situation. Had everything ended with that first date, things would have been fine. If Mandy and Phelix got serious, Mandy could've introduced Molly to him later, and no one would be the wiser. Even after having sex on that first night, the situation could have been salvaged. But now, after two weeks of lunch, him taking care of her, and the amazing evening they'd just had, Molly wasn't sure things could be fixed. For one, she really wanted to see Phelix again, and she was starting not to care that he was her sister's boyfriend.

Phelix was everything Molly had ever looked for in a guy; sweet, caring, a good sense of humor, smart, and he seemed to enjoy the same things she did. Trying to figure out how Phelix and her sister had gotten together boggled Molly's mind.

Mandy was smart, but Molly didn't see how she and Phelix fit together. Mandy would have missed the literary reference on the food. She wouldn't have been able to sit through four hours of a sci-fi show, much less laugh about the differences between the old series and the new series. Music videos and daytime TV were more to Mandy's taste. Her sister and Phelix liked very different thing, and Molly could easily see how those differences could come between them over time. She had much more in common with Phelix than Mandy did.

An idea struck Molly, and she paused in her train of thought. *Of course!* Mandy had found a male version of her twin. An opposite to her personality. Someone that she could fight with and then have amazing makeup sex with. Molly groaned out loud as she fit all the pieces together. Mandy would never be happy with someone with her own personality. She needed someone to take charge, to show her how things were done, to take care of her when she needed it. As the oldest, it had always been Molly's job to take care of her younger sister. True, they were only 2 minutes apart, but she had always been more responsible than Mandy.

Molly got up from the couch, pissed that she hadn't made this connection before. Her feet worried the floor as her mind churned. She was going to have to find a way to squash her feelings for Phelix. There was no way she could come between Phelix and her sister now. Mandy needed someone to take care of her. She *needed* a male version of Molly. Molly chuckled as she thought. Maybe Mandy would listen to him better than she listened to Molly.

All of her life, Molly had tried to expand Mandy's horizons, but the woman was perpetually into what was popular at the moment. Maybe Phelix could make Mandy's world more than the most trendy styles and hottest clubs. All Molly had to do was find a way to forget about the amazing man that had rocked her world with his every kiss. She blew out a breath knowing it probably wasn't possible to burn him out of her heart now. The time they shared had seared him in there pretty good.

A horrible thought made her stop. She'd had sex with Phelix last night, twice. Both without protection. Fear raced up her spine. Rushing to her bedroom, she ripped open her dresser looking for something she could wear out of the house. She needed to get down to the local pharmacy. The last Plan B pill had forced her to have her period a week early, but she didn't want to risk the chances of getting pregnant with Phelix's child. That would really throw a wrench into any plans Mandy might have.

Stuffing her feet into her shoes, Molly located her keys. It had been five years since she had been on birth control pill, and now she was going out for emergency contraception for the second time in a month. She just hoped that the pharmacist wouldn't think too badly of her. Maybe she should get a box of condoms just in case. She could always tell Phelix that she had forgotten to take her pills that day. Molly shook her head and decided against it. Mandy would see to it that they never got used. Anyway, with his size, what type of condoms would Phelix wear?

MANDY SAT DOWN ON MOLLY'S COUCH AND PICKED UP the throw pillow. She toyed with the plush object before tucking it into her lap. She felt bad about coming so late on Sunday since they both had to be up for work in the morning, but she couldn't wait to tell her sister what had happened. "You don't have to worry about Phelix anymore."

Molly raised an eyebrow at her sister. "You told him the truth?"

Mandy fidgeted with the tassels on the pillow. "Not exactly," she said, squirming in her chair. She had gone over to visit Phelix as soon as she'd gotten back to see what she could do about their problem. "I told him that I thought his visits could cause problems at work."

Molly's face went blank "Mandy," she protested, "he knows Mr. Baker."

"Exactly," Mandy said, tucking the pillow back in the corner of the couch. "If he knows your boss, it could get out that you're not me. Anyway, what are the girls in your office going to say?"

"Oh, I'm sure there's going to be hell to pay on Monday," Molly grumbled. "One of the girls saw Phelix taking me out on Wednesday. I suspect there will be a lot of questions to answer when I get back in." She sighed. "I love those girls, but, man, they can't keep their mouths shut to save their lives."

"See," Mandy said, spreading her hand out as if she was handing her sister the answer to all of their problems. "Now all you have to do is tell them that he's my boyfriend and everything will be fine."

Molly shook her head. "Think about that for a moment," she stressed. "Phelix has been in to see Mr. Baker at least twice while I was sick. If I tell the girls that he is your boyfriend, it could get back to Mr. Baker. And if he knew Phelix by sight, then there's a possibility that he might see him again. Mr. Baker telling Phelix about our switch would be infinitely worse than him finding out from you. You need to tell him the truth."

Mandy grimaced as the thought rolled around in her head. "I see what you mean." The idea of Phelix finding out scared her, but him finding out through someone else would definitely put an end to what she had going on. She wasn't ready for that yet.

"Tell him," Molly insisted again. "So he doesn't find out some other way."

Mandy sighed. Molly had a point that couldn't be argued with. "I will." She hung her head in defeat. "I promise, but not just yet. I don't want him to be mad about this." She was going to have to find a way to break the news to him gently.

Molly let out a sigh, but didn't push the subject. "So tell me about your weekend."

Grateful for the change of subject, Mandy jumped on the chance to share how amazing her experience at the health spa had been.

Fourteen

Monday was just exactly what Molly expected. The vultures in her office descended upon her as soon as she came through the door. They wanted to know all about the handsome man that had taken her home on Wednesday. Forcing a smile to her face, she told them he was just a friend looking out for her. It was Mr. Baker's reaction that surprised her the most. She expected to get some kind of reprimand over the two and a half days she'd missed, but he barely even mentioned it. The really weird part was when he let her go without asking for some kind of doctor's excuse. The fact that he welcomed her back with a gentle word and a new stack of files disturbed her, but she didn't dare poke the beast.

Lunch time was a little disappointing. True to his word, Phelix didn't come to take her out. A note of sadness overshadowed Molly's heart as she walked herself down to the little café on the corner where she and Phelix had their first lunch. She claimed the same booth they'd taken on their first date and ordered a Reuben. Staring at the empty seat across from her, she wallowed in her misery.

She missed Phelix.

Over the weekend, Phelix had spent a lot of time talking with her over texts. It started with a little message at lunch time on Friday. Their banter had continued throughout the day with each text growing in length, and ended with a lengthy phone call late in the evening. The next morning, she woke to the ping of his good morning message, and they continued chatting almost nonstop all day. At times, it had been difficult to answer his questions about the yoga camp's activities, but, having spent hours listening to Mandy prep for the weekend, Molly was able to make up some believable stuff. Sunday had been a lot of the same. It had brought a strange pleasantness to her empty weekend.

Pulling out her phone, she flipped through the banter that they had shared during that time. Her heart hurt as she looked at the time stamp on the last message. She hadn't received a single word from him since shortly before her sister had come by on Sunday. Her finger hovered over the reply button on his last message. For a moment, she longed to send him a message asking him how he was, but curled her finger away from the screen. She slipped her phone back into her purse, and turned her mind to her sandwich. She needed to find a way to push him out of her life and let her sister be happy. It was the right thing to do. Molly blinked back the tears burning her eyes and turned her full attention to the sandwich in front of her. For some reason, the normally delicious food had no flavor today.

MOLLY GLANCED AT THE CLOCK, WAITING FOR THE END OF the day to roll around. Today had been just as uneventful and sad as yesterday. She'd started the Tuesday with renewed spirits and good hopes, and everything had been fine until lunch rolled around. Molly powered through her disappointment at Phelix's absence, but things took a turn for the worse after lunch when Mr. Baker dropped a stack of files on her desk.

At first, she didn't think anything of it and buried herself in work. After the first few pages, a name grabbed her attention. Fairlane. Molly immediately picked up the file and read through , thinking it was Phelix's medical records. But the information in the file was on a child. The doctor's name was Fairlane. She laughed at her foolishness and went on to enter the information, but the whole stack of files was from Fairlane's office.

Every time she opened a file and found that name, it would tease her with thoughts of the man she couldn't have. After a while, she wanted to go find this Doctor Fairlane and punch his face in for causing her misery.

A sliver of memory worked its way into Molly's head as she entered the information into the billing system. Didn't Phelix say he had a brother who was a doctor? Could that have been what brought Phelix to her building? She spent the rest of her day catching the name Fairlane on her paperwork. She was going to have to find out who this doctor was and tell her sister. If he was somehow related to Phelix, they might have bigger troubles on their hands.

Molly picked up her phone to text her sister, but remembered that she was going to be meeting up with Phelix tonight and dropped the phone down without even unlocking it. Molly made a mental note to stop by the store for a pint of Phish Food ice cream. It was about the only thing that made her feel better when she was this depressed.

LEANING AGAINST THE RAILING FOR THE HANDICAP RAMP,

Mandy stared into the lobby of her sister's building with bated breath. She'd left her own job early to come take her sister out to lunch, but that wasn't the only reason she was here. She rubbed the top of her black gladiator sandal on the back of her leg trying to squash her nerves. Was Phelix going to keep his promise?

Most of her fears lifted when she saw the elevator open up and her sister come out. Mandy clicked her tongue in disappointment in Molly's drab fashion sense, and wondered why Phelix never mentioned the differences between their styles.

Adjusting the strappy black bralette and bright red top, she pushed away from the railing and went to meet her sister. There was a depressed look on Molly's face that tugged at Mandy's heart.

A look of confusion passed over Molly's face, but it was quickly replaced with a smile. "What are you doing here?" she asked as she drew Mandy in for a hug.

"I came to take you to lunch," Mandy answered. She had seen the stress and heartache her sister had been going through, and it hurt Mandy to know that she had a hand in it.

Molly laughed. "That's sweet of you," she said as she turned down the street.

Mandy fell into step next to her sister.

"Did you take off work just to come hang out?"

Mandy heard the suspicion in her sister's voice. Shrugging, she admitted the truth. "I have to admit, it wasn't just to see you."

Molly chuckled. "You were coming to see if Phelix was keeping his word."

Mandy nodded.

The sigh Molly let out hurt Mandy's heart. "Well, you'll be happy to know that I haven't heard a single peep out of him since Sunday afternoon." She pulled open the door to the local deli and held it for Mandy to enter.

Mandy considered her sister as they went inside and ordered food. The set in Molly's shoulders was solid, but Mandy could see the pain and distress Molly was in. "Does it really bothering you that much?"

Molly sighed, took her food, and turned away from Mandy to find a table.

Mandy chewed on her lip as she took her soup from the server and followed her sister to the table.

"Honestly," Molly said as she stared at her pastrami sandwich, "yes."

Going deathly still, Mandy held her breath and waited for her sister to continue. She'd known there were going to be issues, but she didn't think things had gotten this bad.

"I know that it was only a short time, but I really got to like him," Molly admitted. "I miss his company."

Mandy's lips pressed into a hard line as anger bubbled up inside her. She had done her best to keep her anger in check, even when her sister had slept with her boyfriend, but this was starting to sting of betrayal.

An unhappy look crossed Molly's face and she shook her head before Mandy could say anything. "Stop," she warned. "I'm not going to steal your boyfriend. I'll get over this, just give me time." She turned her attention away from Mandy, and started picking at her sandwich.

Mandy stared at her sister for a long moment. She could see the despair riding her sister, and it made her heart hurt worse. She hadn't meant for any of this to happen. Reaching out, she took up her sister's hand and squeezed it.

"I'm sorry."

Molly met her gaze. Anguish darkened her eyes.

"I didn't know things had gotten that far out of hand."

Anger flashed in Molly's eyes. "I told you I was starting to like him," she snapped, ripping her hand from her sister's. For a second, Mandy was sure her twin was going to hit her, but Molly clenched her fist and folded her hands in her lap. After a few long breaths, Molly met Mandy's eyes again. "I knew I was starting to like him, but I thought it would go away if he stopped coming around." The sigh she let out carried a world of sadness in it. "I just didn't realize I'd miss his company so much."

The angry spot in Mandy's heart melted. "Oh Molly," she sighed as she picked up her spoon and stirred her soup around. "I don't know what to do." She had done her best to stop Phelix from coming around, but she still hadn't told him the truth about what had happened. And she had no idea how to mend her sister's broken heart.

"There isn't anything to be done," Molly said. "Just give me time. I'll get over this." She glanced up at her sister through narrowed eyed. "But don't expect me to be happy with you for a while."

Mandy chuckled. It may take Molly a while for to forgive her, but she knew her older sister would always be there for her. "I really am sorry about this. It was never supposed to go this far."

"It's fine," Molly reassured her. "Finish your soup before we're both late getting back to work."

Mandy smiled and turned her attention to her food. It was clear to see that her sister was done talking about the issue. Now, all Mandy had to do was make sure Phelix didn't fall back into the habit of lunch. She stirred her soup around thinking about her man, and trying to come up with ways she could keep him occupied during the day. Maybe she could talk with her boss and get an extra-long lunch so she could stop by and visit him.

When they were done with their food, Molly cleared off the table and headed back toward the door. "Thanks for lunch," she said as Mandy fell into step with her

"Are we okay?" Mandy asked not sure if her sister was ready to forgive her.

"Yeah, we're good," Molly sighed. "Just keep your boyfriend to yourself."

Mandy chuckled and agreed as she hugged her sister. Letting her go, she watched as Molly disappeared back into her office building. Tugging her pencil skirt into place, she set off to catch the train across town. If she hurried, she might still have time to meet up with Phelix for a late lunch. Seeing her sister's misery had almost been enough for her to agree to tell Phelix the truth. She needed to feel his touch and remember why he couldn't lose him to some stupid lie that had gotten out of control.

THE LARGE VASE TOOK UP MOST OF THE FREE SPACE ON Molly's desk. She sighed deeply and glared at the two dozen red roses mixed in with baby's breath and silver curly sticks. They were amazingly beautiful, and they were not what she needed this Friday morning.

Molly didn't need to look at the card to know who sent the roses, but she plucked out the envelope and broke the seal anyway. The card was romantic. Her heart clenched as she read the flowery words printed on the inside, but it was what had been handwritten that made Molly's chest constrict and tears come to her eyes.

Hey Beautiful, I finally understand. Please accept this gift as a token of my apology. Two dozen roses. The first, for the issues I've caused. I'm sorry, and I promise to make it right. The second, for the most wonderful woman I know. I have missed our lunch times together and look forward to seeing you this evening. Until then, enjoy.

With trembling fingers, Molly read over the scrawling handwriting. The loving words intended for her sister made her heart ached. Tears burned her eyes, threating to spill down her face. An overwhelming urge to destroy the gift flowed through her. She wanted to hurl the loving present across the room and watch as the crystal vase shattered against the wall; to tear the sentimental words into little bits of confetti and toss them out the window, where the wind would scatter it to the corners of the world. Instead, she settled for folding the card up and moving the vase of flowers to the top of the filing cabinet where she wouldn't have to look at them.

Sitting down in her chair, Molly pulled out her phone to send her sister a text to find out what to do about the gift. Molly took a quick picture of the vase and card, and sent it off to Mandy. Glancing over the card once more, Molly read through the feelings written in those words again. Something seemed off with what Phelix had written. What did he finally understand? If he suspected something wasn't right between he and Mandy, wouldn't he have spoken about it with Mandy face to face? And if Phelix had found out about her and Mandy switching places, why would he send her roses as an apology? Wouldn't he be upset by it? Molly looked up at the vase again. Her eyes studied the gentle curve of the clear glass holding the flowers, but paused as something caught the light. She stood up to get a better look at the object wrapped around the neck of the vase.

Molly gasped at the row of diamonds sparkling against the glass. She glanced around her office to see who was there. It was still very early and the biggest gossips hadn't made it in yet, but she could see some of the other girls exchanging whispers. Reaching up, she pulled on the ribbon holding the tennis bracelet to the vase. The bracelet slipped loose into her hand. Clutching the jewelry, she sat back in her chair to look at it. How could he leave something like this just sitting on her desk? Molly looked around again before pulling the ribbon away from the diamond and gold chain. Running her fingers over the sparkling gems, she noticed a small tag near the clasp with *My Beautiful* stamped into it. Molly drew in a deep breath trying to keep the words from stinging. She squeezed the bracelet in her hand trying to cool her anger. That was the pet name Phelix was always calling her. The fact that he used it with her sister hadn't sunk in before, and the realization that he did brought tears to Molly's eyes.

Resisting the urge to throw the bracelet away, she wadded it up and glanced around again trying to think. She didn't want anything to happen to it, but she didn't have a pocket to hide the thing away in, and dropping something that expensive into her purse just didn't seem safe. She considered tying it back around the vase, but leaving diamonds out was much too tempting.

Molly looked around her office one more time before opening her hand and considering the thin band. Sitting up defiantly, she wrapped the bracelet around her wrist and clasped it into place. Damn it, Phelix had sent it to her office, so she was going to wear it until she had the chance to see her sister. And, if the card meant anything, it would probably be tomorrow or later. She looked up at the roses. A malevolent smile slipped across her face. Phelix may have sent them to her sister, but they were beautiful and Molly was going to claim some of them for her own.

Half of the long stem roses were an apology for troubles caused. Molly definitely considered those hers. Phelix had been coming to her work, causing her problems, not Mandy. Molly decided that once she got the bouquet home, she was going to pull out the twelve prettiest to keep. Her twin would just have to suck it up.

Giving her wrist a sharp twist, Molly savored the feel of the metal sliding over her skin. A deviant smile crept onto Molly's face as she slipped the card into her purse. Maybe she should just keep the bracelet too. She deserved something nice for all the troubles and heartaches the entire situation had caused her. After all, it fit her perfectly. Looking at the sparkling object one last time, Molly shook her head. No matter how upset she was with the situation, it would be wrong to keep a gift intended for her sister. It would find its way there eventually, just not today.

Fifteen

A knock on the door interrupted Molly's enjoyment of her ice cream. Grabbing the TV remote, she paused her movie before getting up from the couch. She really wasn't expecting anyone tonight.

Molly glanced at the clock. It wasn't very late. Maybe Mandy was coming up to collect the roses before she headed off to see Phelix for the evening. Molly licked the traces of the chocolate ice cream from her fingers. As she crossed the room, she decided what to say to her sister. Getting the vase home on the subway had been hell and she hadn't taken the time to separate out the twelve rose that she was going to keep. She yanked the door open ready to tell her sister to bugger off, but snapped her mouth shut on the insult. "Phelix!" Molly squeaked instead. "What are you doing here?"

Phelix chuckled. "I told you I would see you

this evening," he said, looking at Molly expectantly.

Molly stood in the doorway and stared as her brain tried to piece everything together. Wasn't Mandy meeting Phelix at a restaurant this evening?

"Can I come in?" Phelix asked.

"Yes," Molly squeaked. Stepping back, she let him into her living room, trying to think of a way to salvage the situation. Her sister was going to kill her when Phelix didn't show up at the restaurant. "I thought we were meeting at the restaurant for dinner?"

He grinned. "In that case, you're late," Phelix teased. Reaching out, he touched the side of Molly's face. "You look wonderful tonight, beautiful." Leaning in, he placed a soft kiss on her lips. The light pressure of his kiss pulled a soft noise from Molly, and the corners of his mouth curled up in pleasure. Deepening the kiss, he wrapped her up in his arms and pulled her against him.

The door slipped from Molly's hand as she melted into his kiss. It had swung mostly shut by the time he pulled back from her lips.

Licking his lips as if he had just eaten something tasty, he gave her another quick kiss. "You taste like chocolate," he said as he let Molly go. "I like it." Turning from her, he made his way into the living room.

When Molly's brain cells started firing again, she shut the door fully and turned around to watch her unexpected guest.

Pulling off his tie, Phelix dropped both it and his coat down on her loveseat before claiming a place on her couch. "So what are we watching?" he asked as he rolled up his sleeves.

Molly's stood there in shock until Phelix picked up her pint of Phish Food ice cream and started digging out one of the dark chocolate fish. "Hey!" she cried, going over to reclaim her treat. She didn't know what to do with Phelix, but she drew the line at letting him eat her frozen comfort.

Phelix stuck the fish and spoon into his mouth before grabbing Molly's outstretched hand. With a quick jerk, he pulled her off balance and caught her before she could fall. Spinning her around, he brought her down to the couch beside him.

The move had been too fast for Molly to fight. Leaning against the curve of his body, she froze as his arm came down, pinning her in place.

Pulling the spoon out of his mouth, he kissed the top of her head and held the ice cream out for Molly to take. "So what are we watching?" he asked again.

Molly looked at the pint and then up at him in bewilderment. Things were not adding up in her brain. Why was he here and not waiting for her sister? "*Die Hard*," she said, taking the paper carton from his hand. She had to find a way to get away from him and let her sister know what was going on.

"Good choice," Phelix said as he shifted under her and slipped his shoes off. "Are you going to start it back up?" he asked, looking at the remote control sitting on the coffee table just out of his reach.

Confused, Molly answered him. "Um... Okay." She sat up and got the remote control. With her thumb on the play button, she stopped and looked over at him. "Wasn't the plan to go for dinner?" Mandy was going to be really pissed off that Phelix was here and not waiting at a restaurant for her. If she could get away from Phelix for just a few minutes, she could get a hold of her sister and let her know what was going on.

"We can go to dinner if you like," he said. "But I'd much rather be right here." Phelix pulled Molly in so she was leaning against him again. "Besides, you're not dressed for dinner." His eyes traveled over her extra big t-shirt and sweatpants.

Molly blushed. Mandy would never be caught dead in anything like this. "I should go change." She tried to get up, but Phelix held her down.

"Don't." He nuzzled his face into her hair. "I

think you look absolutely amazing."

Molly's blush deepened as he took the remote control from her hand.

"Besides, you'll miss the movie." Phelix hit the play button and unfroze the screen.

Molly sat there, torn. How was she supposed to explain this to her sister?

Phelix wiggled again and relaxed back into the couch, pulling her to rest against his side. He held the spoon out to her.

It took her a moment to register the shiny object waving in front of her face. Reaching out, Molly took the spoon and leaned back into his side, accepting the fact he wasn't leaving. She would have to come up with something to tell her sister, but there was nothing she could do about it now.

Phelix made a pleased noise as he draped his arm over her. His hand slid down across her stomach as they watched the movie.

It took Molly a while to fully relax against Phelix. She knew it was wrong, but she really enjoyed his company. Molly scraped up a bite of the marshmallow swirled in the chocolate and stuck it in her mouth. Phish Food was the ice cream she ate when she was feeling depressed. With the warmth from Phelix's body easing the pain she had been feeling since Sunday, she really didn't feel like eating much more of the sticky sweetness. She scraped another fish from the mess and looked up to the man cuddling her. Lifting the treat up, she held it out for Phelix to take.

He chuckled before licking the ice cream from the spoon.

A happiness that she hadn't known all week slid over Molly as they cuddled on the couch and shared her ice cream.

"I LOVE THAT MOVIE," PHELIX SAID AS THE CREDITS SCROLLED across the screen.

Molly sighed as she cuddled under the throw she'd pulled down during the movie. Mandy didn't enjoy action movies and wouldn't have made it through the classic flick. Molly cuddled against Phelix as he toyed with the string of diamonds wrapped around her wrist.

"I see you found your present," he said as he slipped his finger under the band, drawing her attention to it.

Molly blushed, glad that her sister hadn't made it up to get the flowers. Things might have been different if she had told Mandy about the diamond band. "It's very nice." A pained smile passed over her face as she looked at the ring of gold and diamonds that she was going to have to give up soon.

"It makes me happy to see you wearing it," Phelix said, raising her hand up and kissing it. "So what would you like to do now?" He smiled at her suggestively.

An array of emotions shot through Molly as Phelix leaned over and found her lips. She loved the way his kisses made her heart pound. A million reasons why she should stop him bounced around her brain, but she ignored them. She wanted him too badly to pull away. Molly tilted her head back to give him easier access to her mouth. She loved the way he tasted, all warm and sweet on her lips.

Phelix deepened the kiss, driving little tendrils of anticipation deep into her body.

Molly moaned as his hands shifted downward, slipping up under her shirt. The heat from his palms felt good on her bare skin. She rolled over in his arms to face him more.

He slid his hand up her back under her shirt and groaned in anticipation when his fingers slid all the way up her back without meeting the usual resistance of a bra. Holding her tighter, he worked her mouth more passionately.

Following the lead of his hands, she slid up to sit in his lap. She knew it was going to cause problems, but under the delicious pressure of Phelix's lips, she didn't care.

With a soft pat, he broke their kiss long enough to turn her.

Molly moved across his lap, so her knees slid up alongside his legs. She straddled his lap as he let out a soft groan and pulled her toward him for another toe-curling kiss that left her breathless and wanting for more than just air. Pulling back, she drew in a great breath.

Lacking her mouth, Phelix laid a line of kisses against her skin.

She tangled her fingers in his hair as he ran a line of nibbles and kisses down the side of her neck to the hollow of her throat. Leaning her head back, she closed her eyes, savoring the pleasure he pulled from her body.

Phelix pushed the loose t-shirt up and over Molly's head exposing her soft flesh to the cool air of the apartment.

Taking the shirt from him, she pulled it free of her arms and dropped it on the floor behind her. Shaking her head, she shifted her loose hair back out of the way. Molly shivered as Phelix ran the tips of his nails down her back.

His hot mouth found the mound of her breast, and he worked his tongue over her nipple. He plucked her other nipple to a hard point before switching sides to soothe it.

Holding his head to her, Molly tilted her face down to rub her cheek into his hair. She drew in a deep breath, taking up the spicy scent she'd come to love. A touch of sadness bloomed in her heart, and she sighed into his hair. She had to find a way to stop him. She'd spent the whole week nursing her broken heart. Letting him continue would only lead to more heartache and pain.

Sensing the change in her feelings, Phelix pulled back from his exploration and leaned back to capture her lips again. His hands ran down her body to her hips. He moaned into her mouth as he tilted his hips up and pulled her down against him, fitting them together.

Molly could feel him rubbing up between her legs, hard and ready for her. Another shiver of anticipation ran through her body. She tried to tell herself she wanted him to stop, but the lie wouldn't sink in. The feel of him pressed into her set Molly on fire. There was only one thing that could quench the lust riding her. She knew it was going to be painful, but the temptation to continue was too great. A smile curled her lips as a delicious idea passed into her mind. Placing her hands on his chest, she pushed back from him, breaking their kiss.

Phelix's breath came hard and fast as his fingers dug into her sides, pulling her against him.

The lust in Phelix's crystal blue eyes made Molly's already heated flesh redden more. Scraping her nails over the material, she started in on the little buttons of his shirt. Shifting back, she worked open his dress shirt and was slightly disappointed when she found that he was wearing a t-shirt under it, but that didn't stop her from her goal. Leaning forward, she pushed away from him and let the line of her body rub against his groin as she slid from his lap and between his legs.

Phelix moaned as she fondled him through his pants.

Pulling out his shirt, she kissed his stomach just above his waistline. His breath caught as she licked the space between his belly button and his belt line, but she didn't look up to meet his eye.

Making short work of his belt, she eased his zipper down. She could feel him watching her, but she kept her eyes on her task as she eased him out of his pants. It had been a while since she had done this, and she was afraid she would lose her nerve if she knew what emotion he held in his eyes.

Molly took him in her hand gently and swallowed the saliva building in her mouth. Rolling her lower lip into her mouth, she licked it before leaning in and rubbing the wet surface over the tip of his swollen length. She blew on the damp skin before running the flat of her tongue up his shaft.

Phelix shivered. He groaned as Molly opened her mouth and took him in.

Molly glanced up when his fingers sunk into her hair. The look of pure ecstasy covering his face sent a thrill of satisfaction through her. Pulling him further into her mouth, she worked him over for a while trying to discover what he likes. He tried to keep his breathing even and steady, but she kept hitting one very sensitive spot that drew small gasps from him. Smiling, she nibbled that area again, earning another pant from him. Slipping her fingers into the waistband of his pants, she pulled on them.

Phelix lifted his weight from the couch, letting her slide his pants over hips.

Tugging on them, she pulled his pants down to pool on the floor around his ankles. Now that she had found his buttons, it wouldn't take her long to drive him to his release, and she wanted his clothing safely out of the way. Running her hands up the inside of his thighs, she focused on giving him pleasure. She played around with him for a while longer, avoiding overstimulating him too much. Once she was sure he couldn't take anymore, she went back and licked that one spot that kept making him gasp. Smiling, she licked it harder.

"No!" Phelix's hand clamped onto her head, stopping her action before she could bring him to his peak. He forced his breathing to even out before releasing her. "You're going to make me cum doing that."

Molly smiled and caught his length up between her shoulder and cheek. "Isn't that the point?" She grinned as she nuzzled him.

Growling, he pulled on her shoulders, lifting her up to him.

She giggled and bent to his will.

Phelix yanked the back of her sweet pants down nearly ripping them from her body.

Laughing, Molly helped him with the rest of her clothing.

Sliding his hand between her thighs, he ran his fingers up into the folds of delicate skin. Phelix made a pleased noise as he pushed around the slick wetness seeping from her.

Molly braced her hands on his shoulders while he explored her depths with those talented fingers. When Phelix tilted his head up, she leaned forward to give him the kiss he wanted. To her utmost surprise, he pulled her hard against him, crashing their lips together. Having lost her balance, Molly fell to his lap.

Catching her, he guided her down so that she ended up straddled over him again. He wasted no time in getting her hips high enough for him to find her and pulled her down on him.

Molly moaned as he pushed his length up and filled her.

Phelix pulled on her hips until he was seated completely inside of her. He gave her one good hard thrust before setting her into a solid, but gentle rhythm. Wrapping his arms up around her back, he held her close as they moved together.

"Oh, Phelix," Molly panted as he lavished kisses along the skin of her chest and breasts.

Growling, Phelix thrust up in her harder. "Phalen," he whispered against her skin before returning to his smooth rhythm.

Confusion crossed Molly's face, and she pulled away as her brain tried to kick in. "What?" she asked trying to stay in the rhythm he set and think.

"It's Phalen," he restated.

Molly's motions slowed at the words trickled in. "But I thought—" Molly started, but he cut her off.

"Don't think," he growled. His hands dropped to her hips and changed the direction she was moving so he rubbed against her, driving conscious thought from her mind.

The new sensation pushed her closer to that

edge, and she gasped for breath. It only took a few more moments before her world fell apart. She slumped over to his shoulder and breathed the new name he had given her. The hands on her hips tightened, and he pulled her against him one more time before joining her in the orgasm. They twitched together for a while before he laughed. She could feel him twitch deep inside her.

"God, beautiful, I have no control with you." He moved her slightly limp body back so he could kiss her softly. "I love you," he said as soon as their lips parted.

Horror ripped through Molly's body upon hearing those words. A pain deeper than she could remember stabbed into her and tears welled up in her eyes. "Oh, Phelix! I'm so sorry!" she cried and leaned forward to his shoulder to sob hysterically.

He wrapped his arms around her trying to calm her.

Gasping a few times, Molly tried to push the anguish back so she could tell him what her sister should have. "I'm not Mandy. I'm her sister, Molly." She panted, and tried to get up from his lap.

He held her in place. "What?" he said softly.

Molly sobbed again and tried to move away, but he wouldn't let her go. "I'm Mandy's twin sister Molly." She explained and shifted again trying to get free. She could get through this if she could just get him out from inside her.

He held her fast to his lap as he gave her a stern look. "Explain."

Molly sobbed and wiggled trying to get free. "Please don't be mad at us." Seeing that wasn't doing her any good, she stopped struggling and hung her head. She sniffed back as many of the tears as she could before she started into her story. "Do you remember that dinner we had a month ago when I twisted my ankle?" Molly shifted as far away from him as she could get, and looked at one of the buttons on his shirt unable to meet his eyes.

"Yes," he said softly.

"Mandy asked me to go in her place that night." Molly looked up into his face. It was surprisingly blank as she went on with her tale. "She had come down with the stomach flu."

"The one you had last week?"

Molly nodded.

"Go on."

"She came to me begging me to go to dinner with you. After she had made such a fuss about you breaking dates, she felt she couldn't break that one."

"And you agreed to this?" His words were very level.

Molly would much rather have him yelling at her. She nodded as a sob slipped out.

He paused for a moment before continuing. "Why?"

"She's my sister," Molly cried as she sobbed again. "She was in trouble and needed my help. I told her that I didn't think it was a good idea, but she insisted. We've swapped places many times before, so I agreed. It was never supposed to go this far. The date was supposed to end with a kiss on the front stoop, but Mandy and her fucking heels screwed that up." Molly bent her head back as tears leaked from her eyes. She wrapped her arms around herself feeling very exposed.

"And?"

Molly drew in a shuddering breath and let it out slowly. She hung her head again and let her hands fall to the space between them. "I told Mandy about what happened that night." Finding the hem of Phelix's shirt, she toyed with it trying to relieve her nerves. "She couldn't get mad about it, but she was far from happy. She promised that it was the last time, so I put it behind me." Molly's lip trembled as tears threatened her again. "That is until you showed up in the lobby at work on Monday."

"So why didn't you tell me that I'd gotten you confused with your sister then?"

Molly sighed again. "I don't know." Her shoulders slumped a little. "I was worried about my sister and her relationship. I knew she really liked you and I didn't want to screw that up. Since you just happened to be in the area, I figured the one lunch wouldn't hurt." Molly looked up into his face again. "But you came back on Tuesday. I tried to push you away gently so you wouldn't get mad at Mandy, but that didn't work so well."

"And Wednesday?" he pushed.

"Wednesday I was irritated. It hurt knowing that you had spent the evening before with my sister."

He chuckled.

"What?" Molly asked, indigent that he would laugh at her pain.

"That explains why you were so bitter that day."

Molly huffed at him. "I went home that night and told Mandy to make you stop coming by."

"Why?"

She looked up at the question. "Honestly?"

"We are going for the truth here."

Nodding, Molly let out another deep breath. "I was starting to have feelings for you." She toyed with his hem again. "When you didn't show up on Thursday, I was depressed. I knew it was for the best, but I still wanted to know more about you. I shouldn't have been, but I was actually glad to see you back on Friday." Molly looked up into his face. "Can I get up now?" She didn't want to have this conversation like this. It made her uncomfortable to bare her soul with him buried so deep inside her.

"No." He held her down against him solidly. "Continue."

Molly let out another sigh. "It tore me up, but Mandy assured me that she'd convinced you not to come to lunch anymore. So I was shocked when you were waiting for me on Monday. It made me so happy when you kissed me on the sidewalk. And just the suggestion of getting back in your bed had my heart thumping for the rest of the day." Molly blushed, uncomfortable with the admission. "Of course I told Mandy about everything so that if you mentioned it, she wouldn't be caught by surprise."

He nodded.

"Things got really complicated when I got sick."

The corners of his mouth curled up at the edges. "How so?"

"I'd sent a text message to Mandy letting her know that I was sick and that you were taking care of me. Of course, she was furious about it. She stopped by after work on Wednesday to make sure I was okay, but she left before you could get here."

"Was that before or after you ended up in the

bathroom under a towel?" There was a distinct note of disapproval in his voice.

"During. I was still throwing up when she left." Molly shrugged. "Mandy has never been good with that."

He made an unhappy noise. "And Thursday, when you left suddenly, did you really go to get the mail?" He sounded a little angry.

"No," Molly admitted. "I had to stop Mandy. You had arrived earlier than we had expected and she was on her way up to check on me."

"Up?"

"Mandy lives in the apartment below us."

"Well, that explains where you went and why the mail had the wrong address on it."

Molly cringed, she didn't think he had looked that closely at the apartment number.

"So did you even go on that yoga weekend trip?"

"No." Molly shook her head. "That was my sister's thing. She left on Thursday and got back on Sunday."

He sighed and hung his head.

"God, I'm so sorry. I tried to get Mandy to tell you what was going on, but she wouldn't. She thought that if you knew the truth, you'd be mad at her. This is not something that can easily be forgiven."

"And you thought this pack of lies would make me happy?" This time there was a touch of rage in his voice.

Molly shook her head and scrunched his shirt up in her fingers. "No," she cried. "I knew it was going to cause problems, but I didn't know how to stop it without hurting either of you." Molly strained against his hands again. "Please let me up," she begged.

"No." He squeezed his fingers into her hips until she stopped moving. "And what about this past week?"

"This last week has been the worst week of my life!" Molly snapped as anger burned the pain out of her. "I actually started to hate my sister for her shenanigans! I cried my eyes out every night, and I must have gained ten pounds from all the ice cream." Having had enough of the game he was playing, she struggled on top of him. She was done being the bad guy. Damn it; she was a victim in this whole affair. The laughter coming from him stopped her. She gave him an indignant look; how could he laugh at her pain?

"I forgive you," he said as soon as his mirth died down.

Shock stole over her face as she tried to understand his words.

Seeing the lack of comprehension, he repeated himself. "I forgive you and your sister." The smile fell away from his face as he went on. "But if I ever catch you lying to me again, it will *not* go so well." He lifted his arms up and pulled her forward against his body. "Now for your punishment, I will have you again right now." He moved his hips, so he shifted inside her.

Molly made a pained noise as he drove himself deep inside of her. She nodded her understanding, unable to find words to express her feeling. A weight had been lifted from her heart, and she wanted nothing else than for this man to be inside her.

He found her mouth as he rocked his hips underneath her.

Accepting her exquisite punishment, Molly melted into his embrace and kissed him back hungrily.

He growled out his feelings and moved, so she flipped onto her back on the couch. He drove himself into her again before sitting up and ripping his dress shirt off. He flung it across the room before yanking his undershirt over his head.

Molly moaned slightly as she watched him strip out of the last shreds of his clothing. The look he gave her burnt her to her soul.

Dropping down, he crushed his lips to hers in an almost painful kiss. The note of anger in his kiss was echoed in the way he gripped Molly's hips and rocked them up to give him a better angle for his thrusts. His movements had a sharp edge to them, but the intensity of the pleasure he pulled from her made her moan and push back against him.

"Ever going to lie to me again?" he asked, timing his words to match the way he pounded into her.

"No," she gasped, clinging to him for dear life.

"Ever?" He thrusted harder, emphasizing the word.

"Never," she promised.

"Good," he said as he softened his intensity without slowing the speed.

Molly gasped at the change in his motion and held on as he used the softer thrusts to push her up and over the edge again. She screamed out the orgasm and buried her nails into his back again. This time was unlike any of the other orgasms she had ever had. The intensity sent sparkling colors flashing behind her eyes and nearly made her black out.

He hissed as her nails broke into his skin. Molly's body pulled at him as he thrust into her once more. He moaned out his release and collapsed on top of her.

They lay on the couch for what felt like an eternity as the world around them rebuilt itself. He shifted his weight, so he was no longer crushing Molly, and pulled out of her body.

Molly made a pained noise as her abused muscles protested the movement.

He chuckled and kissed her softly. "Let's switch." He patted Molly's side gently and got up off her.

Struggling to get up, Molly laughed when it took his help for her to sit up.

Pulling her against him, he laid down on his back with Molly stretched out on top of him. They wiggled around for a bit until they were both comfortable. Locating the blanket they'd dropped, he pulled it up from the floor.

Molly helped him spread it over them and relaxed back against his chest. She sighed as she listened to his heartbeat.

He ran his fingers through her hair and down to rub her back lightly.

Looking at the sparkling band around her wrist, Molly let out a forlorn sighed. "I should give this back." She shook her wrist, so the bracelet slid around it.

Raising his hand up, he caught hers. "Why?" he said softly. "I got it for you."

Molly's spine stiffened at his words. "I'm sorry. I can't." She shook her head. There was no way she could keep a present from him. It would hurt her sister. As it was, Molly had already destroyed Mandy's relationship with him.

Phelix squeezed her. "Molly, my beautiful." He held her tightly to him as he spoke. "Now I have something to tell you, too."

Molly rolled her head and made a noise, letting him know she was paying attention.

"I'm not Phelix."

Molly froze as the magnitude of that statement sank in. She shifted to stare up at him in disbelief. "What?"

Amusement twinkled in his eyes. "I'm not your sister's boyfriend."

Molly pushed up from him, so she was looking at him fully. *"What?"* she gasped. "But Mandy was... The picture... What the hell is going on?"

The man Molly knew as Phelix laughed at the shock and surprise on her face. He smiled at her. "I'm not Phelix; I'm his brother, Phalen."

Molly's mouth worked like a drowning goldfish as she tried to wrap her mind around that. "Twin brother!" she gasped as the truth hit her.

Phalen nodded.

"Identical twin brother!"

Phalen chuckled and nodded again.

Molly dropped her head to his chest and stared across the room at the menu on the screen. They had forgotten to turn off the TV when the movie was done. Reaching out, she caught up the remote and killed the power. She dropped the remote to the floor as she looked back up to those crystal blue eyes she loved. "Doctor or lawyer?"

Phalen smiled. "Phalen Fairlane, M.D."

Molly blinked as she put things together. "That explains a lot. You're ...?"

"A pediatrician."

"And your office is in our building!" Molly said flabbergasted.

Phalen nodded again.

"That's why you were in the building on Monday, and how you could join me for lunch every day." She paused as the pieces fell together. "That's also why Mr. Baker didn't question you when you said I was sick." She pushed up from him as another thought hit her. *"I've been doing your billing all week,"* she squeaked. "God, I can't believe how *stupid* I am!" She dropped her head back down on his chest, hiding her embarrassment. "I thought you handwriting looked familiar."

Phalen laughed and patted her on the back. "Don't be too hard on yourself."

Molly sighed and relaxed back into his chest and chuckled. She found it ironic that she was cuddling with someone that she didn't even know, but she needed some answers too. "How?"

"Pretty much the exact same thing that happened with you," Phalen answered with a shrug. "My brother called me out of the blue, begging for a favor I owed him. He asked me to go have dinner with this chick he was dating."

Molly gave him a pointed look, and he shrugged again.

"His words, not mine. Anyway, he said that she had thrown a fit about him breaking their dates, but there was no way he was going to be able to make it that night. There was a big case coming up, and he couldn't get away. Usually, he'd have just let it go, but he must really like your sister."

"That's good to know," Molly said and moved her hands to his chest so she could rest her chin on them.

Phalen rubbed his fingers into Molly's back. "Phelix told me that this girl was, and I quote, somewhat flighty and talkative, but amazing to look at and really hot between the sheets, end quote." He smiled at her.

Molly nodded. She couldn't argue about the first three points. She didn't want to know about the last one. "And what did you find?"

Phalen's smile turned a little goofy. "An amazingly beautiful woman who I thought was somewhat flighty and talkative, who turned out to be hot between the sheets."

Molly blushed at his words. "And she wasn't?"

"I thought so at first, but after the second glass of wine, the flightiness disappeared, and I really started enjoying the conversation." Phalen smiled at her. "Even after finding out you were more interesting than I had thought, I was still going to leave you with a kiss out in front of your building unless you invited me in."

Molly chuckled at him. "What made you change your mind?"

"The fact that you had actually injured yourself."

She grinned. "Couldn't leave a girl in distress?"

"That, and the thigh high stockings."

Molly blushed at his word. She knew her skirt had flipped up during the tumble, but she'd hoped that he hadn't seen up it.

Phalen wrapped his arms around her shoulders and squeezed her against him. "There's something about a woman in thigh highs that just does it for me."

Molly giggled again.

He made a contented noise before continuing. "I'd considered just tending to your wounds and leaving, but the personality that you had carefully built up during dinner shattered away when you got hurt. The woman I saw there was not the same woman I'd had dinner with, and it intrigued me."

"So you slept with me?" Molly asked slightly shocked.

Phalen nodded.

"Because you were intrigued?"

"And once I started touching you, I couldn't keep my hands off you."

Molly raised both of her eyebrows in surprise "Oh, really?"

"Yeah. And, it would piss off my brother."

Molly scoffed at him.

Phalen just shrugged. "There were a lot of things leading up to it, but I guess that doesn't really matter now."

"No, I guess it doesn't." Molly sighed a little depressed. She didn't know what reason she had hoped he would give for taking her to bed, but pissing his brother off had not been one of them.

"I didn't count on the problems that decision would give me."

Molly gave him a confused look. "Did your brother give you a hard time?" She couldn't think of what other problems he could have had because of that one night.

"Oh yes. My brother was furious," Phalen said with a laugh. "But I can handle him; it was you that I couldn't handle." He toyed with the ends of Molly's hair.

She gave him a more confused look.

"When I woke up, you were cuddled up in my arms, so warm and sweet. I didn't want to let you go. I knew that once I left, I would probably never have the chance to see you like that again. For a long time, I considered just going back to sleep, but you told me that you had to get up in the morning for work. So I got up and left."

Molly smiled at him. "I wouldn't think that would be hard with a girl you had just met."

"Neither did I, but it was the whimper you made when I let you go that made me want to stay." Phalen's eyes twinkled in the darkened room.

"I whimpered?" she asked shocked.

Phalen nodded his head. "When I went to slip out from under you. It was the sweetest sound I had heard in a long time, I just..." He let out a deep sigh. "I can't explain it without sounding stupid or corny."

Molly chuckled.

"Once I left, I decided to just put the night behind me and get on with my life."

Molly smiled at him. "Then you ran into me on Monday."

"No," Phalen said. Mirth made his eyes light up. "Then I found your torn stocking in my pocket while I was doing the laundry on Saturday."

Molly stiffened in shock. "You took my stocking?"

"That's the weird thing. I was sure that I'd dropped it on the table next to the box of bandages," he explained. "But, when I was checking my pants before sending them to be cleaned, there it was. I have no idea how it got in my pocket."

Relaxing again, Molly rolled her head, so her cheek was resting on her hands.

Phalen let out a deep sigh before continuing. "I thought about just tossing it. After all, it was torn and slightly bloody, but I just couldn't bring myself to do it. So, I rinsed out the blood and hung it up in the bathroom to dry. For two days, it tormented me. Every time I saw it, I thought of you. The smell of your hair, the sound of your laugh, the feel of your skin against mine; it drove me nuts. I finally ended up folding the thing away into my coat pocket to give back to my brother on Monday. In fact, I was supposed to go meet him in the deli for lunch, but then I saw you in the lobby."

Molly smiled and looked back up at him. "So you ditched your brother."

"Yeah, but he forgave me. If he had gone down and seen us together at the deli…"

"All hell would have broken loose." Molly smiled, playing that scene out in her head. She would have called her sister, and Mandy would have been furious at Phelix.

Phalen laughed and nodded his head. "But that wasn't the only reason I ditched Phelix," he admitted.

"Oh, what else?"

"I wanted to know what was going on with you."

"What do you mean?"

"Well," Phalen paused as he thought how to explain, "Phelix had described your sister as trendy, but the outfit you were wearing, though nice, was not trendy."

Molly looked at him, waiting for more.

"I was sure it was you from the wrapped ankle and scraped up knee, but things just didn't fit together. So I took you out to lunch."

"And?"

"And I discovered that there was a lot more going on than I thought. You laughed at my jokes and stories. I didn't have to explain anything. And, man, the way you were watching me made me crazy. I was just about ready to blow off my afternoon appointments and take you home right then."

Molly chuckled. "I wanted your Reuben."

"My Reuben?" Phalen asked confused.

"The sandwich you were eating." Molly's grin widened. "I love the way that place makes them."

Phalen cocked his head a little in confusion.

"But I thought you were vegan?"

"Oh, hell no. I would die without my meat. My sister is the vegan."

Phalen swatted Molly through the blanket. "There's another lie," he said crossly.

"I'm not the only one who told lies, here," Molly snapped back.

"Point," Phalen returned the anger to her. "But I didn't lie to you after that first day."

Molly pushed up away from Phalen, ready for a fight. "True, but you never told me that you weren't Phelix."

Phalen followed her up, so they were both sitting on the couch. "Molly," he said softly and reached for her. There was a pacifying note to his words.

She pulled away from him before he could touch her.

"I'm sorry." He left his hand hanging between them "We've both made some mistakes here. I don't want to fight with you."

Molly looked at him with angry eyes for a moment longer before closing them and relaxing. She let out a calming breath before looking back at him a little more civilly. "You're right. I'm sorry. I don't want to fight either." She leaned in, so his hand landed on her arm.

Phalen pulled her into him, and wrapped her

up in his arms again. They sat together for a few minutes before Phalen leaned back to where he had been lying.

Molly came down with him and rested her head with his on the cushion.

Phalen held her for a little longer, letting the angry vibes seep away.

"Phelix thanked me for our lunch on Tuesday," Phalen said, picking his story back up. "Apparently your sister showed up to their date in thigh high stockings."

Molly chuckled. "She came up and borrowed some of mine. She doesn't like them very much."

Phalen smiled. "My brother's loss." He rubbed his hand down to Molly's lower back. "I'm just glad you like them."

She giggled at the warm tone of this voice. "Are you going to finish your story?" she asked, caressing the skin on his chest.

"Sure." He pecked her lightly now that she was close enough. "What had you so pissed off on Wednesday?" Phalen asked.

Molly blushed as she thought about that answer. "A little of everything." she sighed.

Phalen waited for her to continue.

Drawing in another deep breath, she tried to explain. "I was irritated that you were there. I'd tried to drop little hints to get you to stop coming, but you ignored them. I'd asked Mandy to tell you to stop, but that hadn't worked either. I didn't want you to touch me. I didn't want you to talk to me. Just the thought of trying to be polite, knowing that my sister had slept with you on Tuesday, made me want to turn around and go back inside."

Phalen let out an amused noise.

Molly lifted up away from him as she remembered her irritation. "And then you took me the deli and got me soup. Yes, the soup is good, but you almost got a knuckle sandwich when you ordered the pastrami."

Phalen laughed at the lively way she explained the day. "So you were irritated with me, and not something my brother had done." He thought about it for a moment. "I guess you really *did* want me to stop taking you to lunch." He sighed unhappily.

Shaking her head, Molly let out a deep breath. "That's not it." She closed her eyes, and leaned forward to touch her forehead to Phalen's. "It's the fact that I was enjoying your company so much. I was going to start having problems holding on to my sanity if you kept hanging around."

Phalen raised his hand to her cheek and tilted his head up to kiss her.

Molly melted into his arms again.

Pulling her with him, Phalen rolled over so

that they were both resting on the couch side by side. "I'm glad you were enjoying my company." He settled the blanket over them as the narrow couch forced them closer together. He wrapped his arms around Molly so one arm cradled her head and the other pinned her to him.

"True, but it wasn't too good for my mind," Molly grumbled. "I realized I had a problem when you didn't show up on Thursday, and I spent the entire lunch time looking around for you."

Phalen snickered at her.

"Laugh it up fuzz ball," Molly huffed.

"I'm sorry." Phalen leaned in and kissed the pout from Molly's lips. "I really did have an emergency on Thursday. A woman brought her son in with a compound fracture in his shin. The poor kid was so scared and bleeding everywhere. I spent most of the morning fixing him up." Phalen shook his head. "And by the time I was done, I'd gotten blood all over my pants and ended up in scrubs. It would have been really hard to try to explain why Phelix had shown up in hospital scrubs."

Molly looked at him horrified. "Why didn't she take him to the hospital?"

"She could get him in to see us faster than an ambulance could get him to the hospital," Phalen explained. "True, we aren't set up for real trauma, but we can handle a few hard cases."

Molly thought about this for a minute. "That would have been interesting to see."

"A compound fracture?" Phalen asked, slightly appalled.

"No," Molly giggled. "You in hospital scrubs."

Phalen chuckled. "I have a few sets at home." He smiled suggestively. "We can play doctor if you like." He squeezed her against him, earning more giggles from her.

"That would be fun." She wiggled in his arms. "But you still haven't told me what gave us away. I thought I was doing a fair job playing my sister."

"Well, I knew there was something going on, but I just couldn't figure it out." Phalen returned to his story. "The more I got to know you, the more I couldn't believe that my brother was dating you. He likes a different type of girl. One that is more, how should I put this delicately?" Phalen paused and looked at her. "You're way too intellectual for my brother's tastes."

Molly giggled. "Oh, so he likes airheads?"

"He likes to be the man in a relationship," Phalen explained. "I don't want to say anything bad about your sister, but he likes the type that can't figure out the remote controls on the TV."

"That would be my sister," Molly said with a laugh. "She calls me up whenever there is a program on that she wants to record."

Phalen chuckled. "Now I see why he likes her." He relaxed and returned to his story. "Apparently Mandy asked Phelix to stop coming by, and he yelled at me for it."

Molly shook her head. "But you blew him off."

"Yeah, I blew him off," Phalen admitted. "My brother doesn't scare me."

Molly snickered.

"By that time I just couldn't get you out of my head. I really wanted to know what was going on. I knew Phelix had spent the weekend with Mandy, and I just couldn't picture you with my brother. It really messed with my head."

"Well that explains some of your actions," Molly said thoughtfully.

"Like what?"

"Well, anytime I mentioned seeing you in the evening, you got angry."

Phalen looked at her shocked. "I didn't think it showed."

"You did a pretty good job hiding it, but it still slipped out around the edges."

"I have to admit, just the thought of him touching you made me want to hit something," Phalen said. "But, there wasn't much I could do about that. It helped that you also seemed a little upset by it."

"I would say 'a little' was an understatement,"

Molly admitted. "Just thinking about Mandy meeting up with you on Tuesday night turned my stomach." She sighed. "You put all of that work into such a nice lunch, and I went and ruined it for both of us without realizing it."

"That was still the best lunch we shared." Phalen kissed her lightly again.

"How so?" Molly asked confused by his actions. Hadn't she ended the meal on a rather bitter note?

Phalen gave her that funny lopsided grin again. "You kissed me on the cheek."

More confusion filled Molly. She didn't understand why that would make him happy. She had kissed Phalen many times before that.

"That was the first time *you* kissed *me*," he explained.

Molly opened her mouth to protest, but stopped. He had given her many one-sided kisses, but that had, indeed, been the first one that she had given him. "I hadn't realized that."

"That one sweet, little peck on the cheek meant more to me than all of the other kisses that we'd shared," Phalen explained. "It showed true feelings for me, not just some part you were playing."

"So you knew that I was not Mandy by that time?"

"I didn't exactly know, but things weren't adding up," Phalen explained. "Things really fell apart when you got sick on Wednesday, and I took you up to the billing office to let Mr. Baker know that you needed to go home."

She sighed. "He called me Molly."

"He called you Molly," he agreed. "At that point, I knew something was really wrong, but I just couldn't figure it out. Was it a split personality? Were you pretending to be someone else for my brother's sake? The possibility of you two being identical twins that switched places never even occurred to me."

Molly snorted in amusement. "It should have."

"Looking back now, it was the most logical explanation, but it wasn't something that you think can happen. There aren't that many sets of identical twins."

"I know what you mean."

"Anyway, I knew I was taking a big chance of you finding out the truth when I gave you my phone number, but I would have really worried about you if you didn't have a way to contact me."

"I did kind of wonder why you felt the need to give me your phone number," Molly admitted. "I was sure you had Mandy's number already, but I figured it was maybe a work phone or something."

"Isn't it funny how we can easily explain away inconsistencies in life?" Phalen chuckled. "Like when I caught you tasting my spaghetti sauce."

Molly blushed. "You saw that!"

"Yes." Phalen nodded his head. "I found it odd that a vegan would try it when it plainly had chunks of meat in it, but I figured you were a little delirious from the fever. When you didn't mention it later, I figured you had forgotten about it, and I didn't want to bring it up and possibly cause a problem."

Molly laughed again. "Did you know Jell-O is not vegan?"

"What?" Phalen asked shocked.

"Yeah. Apparently gelatin has collagen in it."

"Really." Phalen thought about it for a moment. "But you still ate it."

"At that point I didn't know." Molly shrugged. "I told my sister, and she was furious with me."

Phalen chuckled. "When did you talk to your sister about it?"

"She kept texting me throughout the day."

"So did my brother." Phalen laughed. "Every ten minutes he wanted to know what I was doing and if you were feeling better. I ended up turning the ringer off. The voice mails he left were rather entertaining."

"Mandy wasn't nearly that bad." They laughed together for a few minutes.

Phalen watched Molly as he toyed with a strand of her hair. "You know. I was a little upset with you last weekend."

"Why?" Molly could think of lots of possible reasons why.

"Because I knew you were lying to me, but I didn't know how to call you on it." Phalen sighed heavily again.

Molly blushed her embarrassment.

"I gave you a few opportunities to tell me, hoping that you would take them, but you didn't."

"I know." Sadness crept over her face as she answered him. "I wanted to tell you. I even begged Mandy to come up and tell you, but she wouldn't."

"Then why didn't *you* tell me?" Phalen asked. Anger sharpened his words.

"Because it wasn't my secret to tell," Molly huffed, starting to get upset too. "Mandy would have killed me if I told you and ruined her relationship."

"But you told me today." Phalen said tartly.

"Because I couldn't take it anymore," Molly said angrily. "And my sister will kill me when she finds out." A need to hit something bloomed in her, and she pushing on Phalen's chest to get out of his arms. He tightened his grip on her so she wouldn't fall from the couch.

"Molly." He tried to soothe her, but she kept pushing away. In a desperate attempt to calm her before she crashed over into the coffee table, Phalen pressed his lips to her.

Molly froze in her struggles and relaxed into the warm kiss.

"It's all right," he said as soon as their lips parted again. He caressed the skin on her back.

"Is that why you quit coming to lunch?" Molly asked, a little depressed.

Phalen gave her another soft kiss. "No. I went to see my brother on Sunday, and what I saw there made me stop coming to lunch," he explained.

Molly gave him a puzzled look.

"Your sister stopped by on her way home."

Molly's eyes got really big as she took this in. "Oh dear."

"Yeah. Phelix freaked and shoved me into the kitchen. He told me that he would kill me if I came out. So I watched from the hallway as he let Mandy in. I was ready to hit him when he kissed her. Since I was feeling rather pissed off at that moment, I send you a text message. Phelix would have a hell of a time explaining that one. But, I still couldn't figure out how you were fooling Phelix." Phalen let out another deep breath as he went on with his story. "I watched them talk for a while trying to wrap my head around it. Yes, she looked like you and sounded like you, but there was just something not right. I couldn't put my finger on the difference. The longer I watched them, the more I was sure that she wasn't you. I left by the back door shortly after they started making out. I was really confused by my sudden lack of jealousy. I mean, I was ready to hit him for a simple kiss when she arrived, but now that they were really getting hot and heavy, there was nothing."

Molly chuckled a little at the confused look on his face. "So that made you decide not to come to lunch with me?"

"That helped, but it was the text message you sent back that baffled me." Phalen chuckled. "I must have read over that simple message ten times trying to figure out how you sent it to me while I had been watching you make out with my brother."

Molly giggled again. "I can see how that would be confusing."

"It drove me nuts. So I decided not to join you for lunch on Monday. I wanted to see what you were like without me around," Phalen explained. "So… I followed you."

"You followed me?" Molly said shocked.

"And boy was I surprised by what I saw."

"Really?"

"I have to admit, watching you eat the Reuben on Monday posed a whole new set of questions, but it was Wednesday that really threw me for a loop." Phalen explained, amusement flashed in his eyes. "I came down a little early so I could follow you and was shocked to see you standing on the sidewalk outside waiting for something. With the way you were dressed, I thought Phelix might be showing up to take you to lunch. I nearly had a heart attack when I saw you come out of the elevators to meet the you waiting on the street."

Molly giggled at him again.

"I literally had to rub my eyes to make sure I wasn't seeing things. Once I was sure you both were real, the pieces started falling into place and I was pissed. Seething, I followed the two of you as you laughed together. How could you do something so horrible to Phelix? I decided that I was going to call you both on it in the deli. I was going to let you get settled and then walk up to the table and demand an explanation."

Molly blanched at this thought. "But didn't you?" she asked ashamed of herself.

"It was the look on your face that made me change my mind." Phalen caressed her back again. "When I stopped, I was close enough to hear your sister apologizing to you. That shocked me."

"You heard that," Molly squeaked even more embarrassed and tried to hide her face against his chest.

He chuckled again. "Yes, I heard that." Phalen forced her head up so he could see into her eyes again. "And I heard you admit that you liked me and missed my company."

Molly's blush deepened, and she fidgeted in his arms, not sure what to say.

Luckily, Phalen went on with his story. "It took me a while to process it all, but once I put it together, I found that I had a choice to make."

Molly listened intently as he talked.

"The best choice would have been for me to simply walk away." She stiffened in his arms as he explained. "That would have solved a lot of problems. It wouldn't have been hard to avoid you at work, Phelix and Mandy could go back to not having to worry about their secrets, and you could have gotten back to your normal life."

Molly sighed and nodded her head in agreement.

"Or, I could find a way to force this lie out where we can deal with it. Sure it's going to cause both Phelix and Mandy problems, but that means I don't have to lose the most amazing woman I have ever met." Surprise lit up Molly's face, making Phalen laugh. He pulled her in for another warm kiss.

"Does this mean you're not going to leave?" Molly asked, on the verge of tears.

Laughing more, Phalen squeezed her against him. "Of course I'm not going to leave," he cooed then kissed her. "I don't buy jewelry for a woman I'm never going to see again." Phalen ran his hand down Molly's side to her hip. "Besides, I don't think I can stand the thought of someone else touching you like this." He leaned into her and pressed a kiss to her neck as he ran his hand down her thigh, pulling her leg up over his hip.

Molly giggled under his attention, and a growl born in desire rumbled from his chest. She gasped as she felt him start to harden again. He rocked his hips forward until he pressed up against her already exposed flesh.

"Stop!" Molly pushed on him, trying to put space between them, but all she did was rub herself harder against his lower body. "You're going to get me pregnant."

Surprised filled Phalen's face, he laughed and pulled her back to him for a kiss. "It's okay," he cooed at her soothingly and gave her little pecks on the corner of her mouth. "I like kids."

Indignation filled Molly as she registered what he had said. "*What?*" She scrambled to get away.

Phalen laughed as he wrapped his arms around her body and held her close. "It's a joke." He laughed harder as she flailed and kicked at him. "I'm kidding!" After another moment of smacking him about, Molly settled down into Phalen's arms. He just smiled at the glare she gave him. "So I take it you're not on birth control."

"No." Molly huffed at the smile on his face.

"And what were you going to do?"

"I was going to go visit the pharmacy tomorrow."

"Ahh... the 'morning after' pill."

Phalen gave her a more serious look. "Is that what you have been doing?"

Molly nodded shyly.

"Emergency contraception is great idea in a pinch, but there really haven't been many studies on its effectiveness when used multiple times in a month. You really should have said something. I could have had some terrible disease."

Molly turned a little pale.

"Don't worry. I'm clean and I have had all of my shots." He kissed her softly again. "It will be all right. Although I do like kids, I'll get another dose for you from a friend of mine who's an OB/GYN just in case."

Molly let out a sigh of relief.

"Now where were we?" Phalen pressed his lips to hers for another passionate kiss.

She melted under the heat he offered.

A loud gurgling noise bubbled up from between them, and Phalen pulled back.

Embarrassment flushed over Molly's face.

"What have you had to eat tonight?"

She smiled sheepishly. "Ice cream."

Phalen dropped his head down to his chest, and let out a mood killing sigh. "Why don't we find something for dinner?" he suggested. "Do you still have my stuff here?"

"It's in the closet." Molly looked up toward the door where she had hidden his things away.

"How do you feel about pizza?" Phalen carefully extracted himself from between Molly and the couch.

"That's fine, but what about what we were doing?" she asked, not really wanting to stop.

"We have all weekend to get back to that." Phalen bent down and kissed her softly. "Now get up." He pulled on her hand to get her moving. "What would you like on your pizza?"

"Everything." Molly grinned as he helped her to her feet. "Except those hairy, little fish."

"One deluxe with no anchovies." Phalen laughed and swatted Molly on the backside playfully. "Now go get dressed so we can plot our siblings' demise."

Sixteen

A RUSTLE OF SOUND PULLED MANDY'S ATTENTION AWAY from her phone. She smiled as her sister pulled out the chair next to her.

"Thanks for meeting me, Mandy," Molly said as she settled into her seat.

"No problem," Mandy replied, tucking her phone away. "We haven't had been spending much time together recently."

"True," Molly said. She set her phone on the table and picked up her menu. "You've been rather busy with Phelix lately." A knowing smile crept over her face

"And you've been avoiding me," Mandy said, shooting her sister a pointed glare. It had been nearly three weeks since they had sat down for a proper chat.

Molly ignored her twin's glare. "I haven't been avoiding you, I've been busy."

"Molly," Mandy's voice was somewhat curt, "I

know you. You've been avoiding me. Look, I've already said I'm sorry about the whole Phelix thing, but it's been three weeks since he stopped coming to lunch with you." She paused, and softened her words. "Are you still mad at me?" No matter how badly Mandy had messed up in the past, Molly had never held a grudge more than a few days.

Folding up her menu, Molly placed it on the table. She glared at her sister for a long time. "No. I am not mad at you," she said very pointedly. Picking up her menu again, she looked over her dinner options.

The lie in Molly's words hurt. "You *are* mad," Mandy said. She had to find some way to fix the rift between them. "Please, Molly, tell me what I can do to make this right. I don't want you to be mad at me."

Molly's phone made a noise, and she picked it up from the table. After looking at it, she set it back down next to her menu. "I am *not* mad at you," Molly replied and sat up straighter. "But I am rather upset about something."

Hope bloomed in Mandy's heart. "What is it?" she asked, eager to see what she could do to help her sister.

"Did you ever tell Phelix about us switching?"

Dread dimmed that spark of hope. "No," she

admitted. She had been sure this issue had gone away when Phelix had stopped coming by for lunch.

"Well you might want to," Molly said bluntly. "I might be pregnant."

Shock dropped Mandy's jaw. She stared at her sister in disbelief. "You're *what?*" she gasped.

"You heard me," Molly answered. Her phone buzzed again, and she slipped it from the table to her lap.

Anger bubbled up in Mandy. *"How?"* she yelled. A few people around her turned to look at the outburst and Mandy blushed. Lowering her voice she went on. "I thought you'd taken the plan b pill after both times."

"I did," Molly said as she sat up straighter. "Apparently emergency contraception is not as effective when you take it more than once in a month."

Horror sent chills up Mandy's back. "And it's Phelix's?"

The glare Molly sent her could have melted flesh. "I've only slept with one man during the last two months," she huffed.

Mandy just starred at her. This could not be happening.

"If you will excuse me for a moment," Molly said as she stood up. "I have to go to the bathroom." She didn't wait for a reply before heading off through the restaurant.

Unable to comprehend what she had just heard, Mandy watched her sister disappear through the crowd. How could this be possible? What was she going to do? Mandy was strictly against abortion and could never ask her sister to do something so heinous. *How was she going to tell Phelix?* Mandy's mind boiled with unanswerable questions.

"Mandy?"

A familiar male voice tore Mandy from her thoughts. She looked around for the source of the voice praying that she had misheard. Her eyes fell on a very familiar man walking her way.

"What are you doing here, honey?" Phelix walked up to her table and leaned over to give her a kiss.

"Phelix!" Mandy squeaked before he could greet her. She stood up and knocked her chair over. She whipped her head around to look over at the restroom, hoping that her sister was still inside. Things had just gone from bad to worse. She had to find a way to get him out of here before her sister came back and everything hit the fan. "You can't be here," she said as she pulled on Phelix's arm trying to drag him back out of the dining room.

"Wait," he said and planted his feet. His eyes fell to the table and then off in the direction Mandy had been staring. "Are you here with someone?" Suspicion was heavy in his voice.

"No!" Mandy denied fast and hard. *"Yes!"* she squeaked retracting the lie. Lying would just make the situation worse. "It's not what you think!" She pulled on his arm trying to get him to move before he saw her twin.

Confusion and pain flashed across Phelix's face. "Is this why you broke our date?" Phelix asked slightly hurt. "So you could meet up with someone else?" He turned his head toward the restroom again.

"It's not what you think," Mandy protested again. She had to find a way to get him out of here and explain before things got any worse.

The line of his jaw tensed as he narrowed his eyes at Mandy. "Who is he?"

"It's not a guy," Mandy cried.

"Then who is it?" he demanded.

"My sister!" Mandy cried, desperate to get him out of there. "You have to leave now."

"No." Phelix gave his arm an angry wave ripping it from her grasp. "What has gotten into you tonight?" He stared at her, confused. "Why don't you want me meeting your sister?" The hurt and betrayal was heavy in his voice.

Mandy looked back toward the bathroom, praying Molly wouldn't come out for a while longer. "Please, Phelix," Mandy begged. "I promise that I'll explain everything later." She needed time to process what her sister had told her before she broached the subject to Phelix. They were all going to have something to talk about, but she didn't want to do it in public.

A pained look crossed Phelix's face. "I can't," he explained. "I'm meeting someone here too."

Pain stung Molly's heart. This was their normal date night. Yes, she had been the one to cancel this date, but she had a good reason. How could he make time for someone else on their night. "Who?" she demanded.

Phelix glanced around nervously. "It doesn't matter."

Surprised dropped Mandy's mouth open.

"It's no one you know," Phelix explained.

Anger bubbled up inside Mandy. "After what you have done, you have no right to come in here demanding to know who I am meeting and not tell me the same thing," she said to him very flatly.

"And what have I done?" Phelix growled in the same angry tone.

Anger and aggregations moved Mandy's tongue, and she hissed out her accusation in his face. "You got my sister *pregnant!*"

Phelix backed up from her and blinked. "I did *what?*" he asked shocked.

Mandy crossed her arms over her chest. "You heard me."

Bewilderment covered Phelix's face as he took a small step back. "What are you talking about?" he asked. "I've never even met your sister."

Mandy stared at him in horror as chills raced through her blood, raising goosebumps on her arms. She'd revealed her secret without meaning too. Guilt wilted her anger and she let out a deep, raspy breath. "Sit down." She pulled on his arm.

Phelix looked confused, but took a seat at the table.

Mandy righted her chair and sat back in her seat. She'd let the cat out of the bag in her anger, and there was no way she was going to be able to put it back. Picking up her water glass, she took a long sip to wet her suddenly dry mouth.

"What's going on?" Phelix pressed.

She drew in a long, steadying breath to center her thought and prepared herself for her confession. "About two months ago I did something that I really shouldn't have," she admitted. "I asked my sister to take my place at one of our dinner dates."

Phelix stiffened in his seat. "You did *what?*" he said.

Mandy cringed at the shock in his voice, but went on to explain. "I was sick and I didn't want to break our date," she admitted, ashamed of what she had done. She looked down at the table as she went on. "We'd been going through a period where you were too busy for me, and I fussed about it." She looked up to find shock his face. "I couldn't break the date, so I asked Molly to go in my stead and pretend to be me."

Phelix just stared at her.

"It was supposed to be just dinner, but you ended up taking her home afterward."

Phelix's mouth came open.

"The next Monday you ran into her in the lobby of her office and took her out to lunch, thinking it was me."

"But I never had lunch with you," Phelix protested.

"Hi, Phelix."

Mandy looked up to find Molly coming back from the bathroom with a smug smile on her face.

"It's lovely to finally meet you properly." Molly held out her hand for him to shake.

Phelix looked up at Molly. His eyes ran down her before jumping back to Mandy. His eyes flipped back and forth between the identical girls several times. "Twins!" he gasped as he took the offered hand. "You're twins!"

Molly shook his hand before taking her seat. She smiled sweetly at him "Yes," she said. "And I haven't had the opportunity to thank you properly for everything."

Phelix's mouth fell open again. "But I didn't..." He paused as he pulled his eyes away from Molly to look at Mandy. "I never took her to lunch. I swear!"

Mandy stared at him in disbelief. How could he lie to her like that?

"The guy that took me out sure looked enough like you," Molly added, "Would you like to explain to us what is going on?"

Molly's words enflamed Mandy's rage, and she stared at Phelix waiting for him to answer.

Phelix squirmed in his seat. "It was my brother," he said in a panic. "He took you to dinner."

Numbness ran through Mandy's brain while she listened to him lie.

Molly cocked an eyebrow at him, and gave him an incredulous look. "So you expect us to believe that you have a brother that looks just like you?"

"Yes!" Phelix exclaimed. "Phalen. He's *my* twin." He turned and grabbed Mandy's hand. "You have to believe me." His head turned frantically, looking for something. "He is supposed to be meeting me here."

Emotions rolled through Mandy, and she froze in her seat as his words sank in. "*You* have an identical twin?" Mandy said, unable to grasp what away from him and glared.

Phalen laughed and righted himself in his seat.

Putting aside her shock, Mandy turned back to her sister. There was something still bothering her. "Molly," she said, cutting into Phalen's mirth, "So, if you weren't pregnant, why did you tell me you were?"

Molly looked over to her sister and let out a deep sigh. "Phalen and I set you two up to get this out in the open," she explained.

Confusion washed through Mandy. She shook her head and stared at her sister waiting for an answer.

Molly let out another sigh. "There was no way that Phalen and I could have a relationship and try to hide it from you. It would have made the holidays rather interesting. Anyway, we were getting sick of sneaking around, so the only answer was to get the two of you to confess to this whole fiasco."

"But why pregnant?" Mandy asked, still not understanding why her sister had lied about that.

"It was better than some of the other ideas we came up with," Phalen admitted.

"True," she agreed. "Phalen wanted to have us truly switch places and break up with you two."

"What?" Phelix asked shocked.

"The plan was to bring you out to dinner and

tell you each that we had found someone new," Phalen explained.

"Then we were supposed to get up and meet up with each other in a place where you would see, but I was worried that you wouldn't take that well," Molly said as she looked over at her sister. "I know how you can shut down at stressful times."

Mandy held on to her emotions as she nodded. "And you would have been right," she agreed. "I would probably have been too busy crying in disbelief to see what was going on."

"Another idea was to follow you out clubbing and swap partners," Phalen added.

"But I didn't think I could stand an entire night in another pair of Mandy's heels," Molly admitted.

"And I didn't think I could stand watching her in your arms," Phalen growled. He turned a pointed glare at his brother. "I've seen the way your hands wander."

Phelix chuckled. "Point," he agreed. "You could've just come over while we were together one evening."

Phalen gave him an incredulous look.

"Would you have agreed to me coming over while Mandy was there?" he asked.

Phelix looked over at Mandy. "No, I guess not."

"And I didn't want to walk in on you two making out again," Phalen explained. "Once was more than enough."

Mandy blushed. "When did you walk in on us making out?" she squeaked.

"That is something you'll have to talk with Phelix about."

Mandy looked over to her boyfriend. ready to question him. The sudden arrival of their food shut her mouth before she could ask.

"It looks like we will have a lot to talk about this evening," Phelix said after the waiter left.

Mandy let the subject go for now. "I agree," Mandy said as she folded her napkin into her lap. "We both have a lot to talk about."

"Well," Molly stepped in and ended the strange tension building between them, "for right now, why don't we just enjoy dinner?" She picked up her wine glass. "To new beginnings," she toasted. The other three raised their glasses and joined her.

"THAT WAS FUN," MOLLY SAID. SHE SMILED AS PHALEN walked her down the park's lit pathway. The rest of dinner had gone swimmingly.

"Now that I have seen them together, they are perfect for each other," Phalen agreed as he slipped his hand around Molly's back and held her to his side.

"Do you think they will work out their differences the same way we did?" Molly asked. A smile slipped across her face as she remembered that night on the couch.

"If I know my brother, it will be something close to that," Phalen said. He squeezed her into him, and they walked a little farther together.

"It's beautiful out here tonight," Molly pointed out. Peace flowed through her soul. For the first time in their relationship, she felt comfortable walking out in the open with Phalen. She looked up to the sky where the stars were hidden by the city lights. "The only thing that would make it better is if we could see the stars."

Phalen made an agreeing noise. "I've got my star right here," he cooed, rubbing her side again "You are more beautiful than a whole sky full of stars."

Molly giggled. She still wished there were stars out. She let out a sigh, and let the wish go.

"How about I take you out to the countryside, and we can walk under as many stars as you want?"

Molly grinned and leaned into Phalen's side. It was uncanny how closely their minds worked. She let out a deep, contented sigh. "I would like that."

He squeezed her against him. "All right," he

said. "I have this little place just upstate that would be perfect. We can head out there next weekend."

Molly gave him a confused look. "But, I thought you lived in the city."

Phalen chuckled. "I keep a place in the country to get away from everything once in a while," he admitted. "It's not much, but it's cozy, and there are lots of stars."

Molly smiled again. "Okay," she agreed. They walked on for a little while longer in a companionable silence.

As they walked, Phalen caressed his fingers over the fabric on the side of Molly's shirt. His hand slipped lower to her hip, before dropping down to her butt and the back of her upper thigh. "I'm so glad that you like these." He flicked the strap holding her thigh high stockings up. He stopped and pulled her around to face him. "You have no idea what those things do to me." He leaned forward and gave her a warm kiss.

Molly giggled as he pulled back. "I know exactly what they do to you," she said, stepping in to him and toying with the end of his tie. "And you want to know what?"

"What?" he asked, wrapping his arms around her back.

Molly slipped her arms around him and looked up into his eyes. "I'm not wearing anything under them."

Phalen let out a deep, rumbling growl as he pulled her against him and pressed his lips to hers.

Desire rushed through Molly's veins, pushing out a wanton sound. When she felt the first signs of Phalen's arousal growing between them, she rubbed her hips into him, driving their passion on.

Phalen touched his tongue to her lips, and she opened her mouth to let him deepen the kiss. They stood there lost to each other until the need to breathe drove them apart. They both pulled back panting.

"What am I going to do with you?" Phalen asked. He tangled his fingers in her loosened hair, and pulled her head forward to rest against his chest. He kissed her temple softly.

Entertaining ideas flashed through Molly's mind. "Well," she said as she pulled away so she could look at him again. "You could take me home, strip me out of these cloths, and love me all night long," she suggested.

Phalen drew in a deep breath and let it rumble up from his chest. He gave her another soft kiss before pulling away from her and heading them back toward his car. "It will take me longer than one night to love you the way I want to," he said, flashing her a cheeky smile.

"How much longer?" Molly asked, blushing.

"A lot longer," Phalen whispered as he hurried her home.

THE END

Acknowledgements

SOMETIMES, THINGS LEFTS ON THE BACK BURNER COME TOgether better than you expect.

In 2012, I started looking for a publisher for my Kindling Flames series. Unfortunately, it didn't go very well at first. I realized very quickly that my original manuscript was much too long for an unknown author. So, I decided that I should write a much shorter piece and see if I could get that published. White Lies was born.

I sent the new piece out several times, but received enough refusals that I decided it needed something. But, by that time, I'd found a publisher for the first of the Kindling Flames books, so I shelved the new manuscript and turned to the project at hand.

After a few years, and several books, I found myself coming back to this manuscript. Over the years, I'd sent it off to several people to read. Many of them loved it and wondered why I hadn't published it. It was on their insistence that I found time to rewrite it. It took several weeks of hashing about, but I finally came up with a manuscript I was happy with. But, after so many rejections, I wasn't sure the story was worth sending to a publisher.

I sent the new story off to friends for some more beta reading before I tried to self-publish it. One of them through it was good and suggested that I send it off to Changing Tides. So I did. And that, as they say, is all she wrote.

There are a lot of people I need to thank for helping me get this out. Of course I would like to thank my original beta readers and all those that encouraged me to not scrap this project. Sherry for asking me to take it to Changing Tides. Ethan for enjoying it. Dyan for helping me refine the manuscript. And, of course, my family for putting up with me as I worked my way through the original manuscript, the rewrites, and the long hours of editing and polishing. Thank you all.

About the Author

ORIGINALLY FROM OHIO, JULIE ALWAYS DREAMED OF A JOB in science. Either shooting for the stars or delving into the mysteries of volcanoes. But, life never leads where you expect. In 2007, she moved to Mississippi to be with her significant other.

Now a mother of a hyperactive red headed boy, what time she's not chasing down dirty socks and unsticking toys from the ceiling is spent crafting worlds readers can get lost it. Julie is a self-proclaimed bibliophile and lover of big words. She likes hiking, frogs, interesting earrings, and a plethora of other fun things.

happened. Phelix's denial raced through her and she stuck on something that bothered her. "Why did your brother go out with my sister?" she asked. Something wasn't adding up.

"She should ask why he was supposed to be going out with you," Molly corrected her sister calmly.

Anger bubbled up through Mandy again. Molly was right. Phelix was supposed to have met her for dinner that night. Why had Phelix's brother shown up at dinner and not him? "Yes," Mandy snapped. She turned angry eyes toward Phelix. "Why was your brother there?"

Phelix stared at her. His mouth moved for a moment before words finally came out. "I asked him to take my place when I couldn't make it," he explained. "I had a case coming up, and I just couldn't get away, but it was only supposed to be for dinner." He stopped and stared at her for a moment. "Hey. You did the same thing!" he yelled angrily.

"Hey, Phelix."

Mandy looked up as an identical copy of her boyfriend walked up and patted Phelix on the shoulder. She stared at him, unable to believe her eyes as the man walked around the table, and kissed her sister on the cheek.

"Hey, beautiful," he said as Molly stood up and

soothed down his tie. "What did I miss?" he asked as he took the fourth chair at the table.

Mandy stared at the man sitting across from her in disbelief. He was the spitting image of her boyfriend.

"They're just figuring out what happened," Molly said calmly as she picked up her menu and gave it another look.

Mandy looked between the surprise on Phelix's face and the calm way Phalen picked up his menu and opened it.

"Oh good," Phalen said as he looked at the folder. He glanced at Molly. "So are you having the salad again?" His voice held a teasing note to it.

"Good lord, no," she teased back. "I think I need something with a little more iron in it." Her eyes ran down the menu again. "I'm thinking about a nice, juicy steak."

"The mushrooms and blue cheese crumble is fantastic here," Phalen pointed out.

Mandy followed the calm flow of conversation between her sister and her boyfriend's brother. Things slowly fell into place. "Wait," she said, as she found her voice. "You two *knew*?"

Dropping her menu to the table again, Molly turned blank eyes to her sister. "Of course we knew," she snapped, irritation heavy in her voice.

"It's hard to sleep with someone multiple times without figuring some things out about them." She snapped her menu back up between them.

Folding his up, Phalen slipped it under the edge of his plate, and leaned toward his brother. "Oh, and I'm not switching places with you again," he said as he adjusted his chair. "It makes life too complicated."

"But, but…" Phelix stuttered. He glanced between Molly and his brother. "Phalen, what's going on?"

Amusement filled Phalen's eyes. "Apparently, you decided to call in your favor on the same night that your girlfriend got sick and had her sister stand in for her." He smirked at his twin.

Phelix stared at his brother before turning to look at Mandy. "Is this true?"

Unable to bring herself to admit the act, Mandy sat frozen in her seat.

Molly nodded her head. "We had a lovely date, and it would have ended there if Mandy had just let me wear my own shoes." She reached over and smacked her sister in the arm.

The impact shook Mandy out of her shock. "Ouch!" she cried and leaned away from her twin. She rubbed the sting from her arm. "It's not my fault that you can't walk in heels."

"Yeah, but heels shouldn't be that high," Molly

snapped back.

"Ladies, please," Phalen interrupted them, "we are in public, and I think we've caused enough of a scene tonight."

Embarrassment heated Mandy's face, and she glanced over to see that her sister was turning red too.

Phalen turned his attention to his brother. "Have you figured out what you're having for dinner?" He tapped the other man's menu.

Phelix snapped his attention away from the women and looked at the card on the table. "Um," he muttered as he picked up the card.

"Then I suggest you start looking," Phalen prompted. "The waiter will be here shortly." He looked over at Mandy. "That goes for you, too."

Too shocked to argue, Mandy picked up her menu and looked at it without really seeing it. She was having some trouble coming to terms with what was happening.

"So how was your day?" Molly asked.

Mandy glance at her sister as Molly picked up the water glass and sipped at it. She listened as Phalen started into some amusing story about one of his patents, and how the boy's mother had gone online and diagnosed her son with scabies when it was clearly chicken pox. The ease of their conversation amazed Mandy. How could they sit match her sister. She knew what was in store for her later.

Phelix's visage lightened as he shifted his eyes from one sister to the other. "You know, I understand twins, but it's uncanny exactly how close you two are."

Mandy shot her sister a familiar glance. Molly pulled the pin from her hair so it fell around her shoulders similar to Mandy's. Both girls cocked their heads at the same angle and gave Phelix a practiced smile.

The shiver that ran up Phelix's spine was visible. "That's just creepy." He turned his head to look at his brother. "How are we ever going to tell these two apart?"

Phalen laid his hand on the table, and Molly took it up. "I've got mine."

A flash of light caught Mandy's eye. "What's that?" Mandy asked as she tried to see what was wrapped around Molly's wrist.

Molly slipped her hand from Phalen's grasp and held it out so Mandy could inspect the gift. "Do you remember the flowers that were sent to me at work?" Molly asked.

Mandy's brow furrowed as she recalled the incident. "You mean the ones that you refused to give to me?" she said, as she pulled her sister's hand closer to look at the diamond bracelet.

"Yes," Molly confirmed. "This was tied around the vase."

Mandy rubbed her fingers over the diamonds until she hit the little tag. She flipped it over and read the words written on it. "*My Beautiful*?" she questioned the inscription.

"Once I realized that something was up, I stopped calling her by your name," Phalen explained. "But, I couldn't just call her 'hey you'."

Molly laughed at him and pulled her hand back from her sister. "You could have." Molly looked back at Mandy. "He made me promise not to take it off." She took up Phalen's waiting hand again.

"A name tag!" Phelix gasped. "You got her a name tag!"

Phalen chuckled and rubbed his thumb over her knuckles. "It's not like I got her a collar."

Phelix sat for a moment in thought. "No, but that's a great idea."

Molly leaned toward her sister. "Careful, Mandy, next thing we know they are going to want to tattoo names on us," she sassed.

Phalen pulled on Molly's hand and leaned over to kiss her on the cheek. "And I know exactly where I would put my name on you," he said suggestively.

Mandy's eyes widened as her sister flinched

Phalen nodded his agreement, and Molly turned her attention back to Phelix. "So?"

Mandy's insides flipped about as Phelix turned his attention to her. She didn't know how to answer, but her heart leaped when he laid his hand on the table. She wiped hers on her skirt and laid her hand in his. She could see him consider their future and hoped that they could come to some terms. Her heart jumped when he finally spoke.

"I think we have a lot to talk about."

She bit her lip waiting for more. There was warmth in his crystal blue eyes that eased her fears.

"But, I think we can manage to work this out."

Relief flooded Mandy and she relaxed. Biting her trembling lip, she nodded her agreement.

"Just keep at her, brother," Phalen said as he shot his brother a grin. "If she is anything like her sister, she may take some prodding to get the whole truth out of her."

Mandy glanced at Molly to see what he was talking about. A hint of red colored her sister's cheeks.

"Don't worry, brother." Phelix said, drawing Mandy's eyes back to him. His smile darkened into something very suggestive. "I won't stop until I get everything out of her."

Mandy squirmed in her chair and blushed to

and rubbed his hands on his pants. "But I highly doubt either of you are."

Mandy blanched at the sheer idea of being pregnant.

Phelix rolled his eyes. "Only you would think of things like that."

"I'm a doctor. It's my job to think of things like that," Phalen explained with a smile. "You would be surprised how many of my patients were the results of accidents with prophylactics."

"Phalen!" Molly reprimanded him. "That's not nice."

He let out a soft laugh. "It's true."

"It's still not nice," Molly huffed as she shifted in her chair. She turned her attention to the other couple at the table. "So what do you plan to do now?"

Unsure how to answer that, Mandy looked over at Phelix. She didn't know what to think of her relationship now that their secrets were out.

"What do you mean?" Phelix asked.

"Are you two going to try to work this out?" Molly added.

Mandy drew in a concerned breath as she waited for Phelix to respond, but he just sat there staring at Molly.

Molly laughed and leaned toward Phalen. "You're right; they are perfect for each other."

there and banter back and forth when her world had just been turned upside down?

The arrival of the waiter broke into Mandy's swirling thoughts, and she ordered a glass of wine to help calm her nerves. When her sister ordered the same, a thought struck Mandy and she grabbed her sister's arm. "Wait," she cried out stopping the waiter from leaving. She turned wide eyes to Molly. "What about the baby?" Expecting mothers weren't supposed to be drinking.

Mandy's words triggered something in Phelix, and he sat taller in his seat. "What baby?"

Irritated, Mandy turned her attention to Phelix. "Your brother got my sister pregnant."

Phelix glared at his brother. "Is this true?"

Phalen just shrugged nonchalantly and took a sip from him his glass. "I like kids," he said then set the glass back to the table.

The lackadaisical way he talked about bringing a life in to the world made Mandy bristle. She tensed up ready to explode.

Molly's hand landed on hers before Mandy could lay into Phalen. "Chill, Mandy," Molly said. "He's a pediatrician. Liking kids is in his job description."

Mandy glanced from her sister to Phalen.

Phalen just smiled and shrugged.

Mandy tensed as anger boiled insider her.

Molly patted her sister's hand again, and rolled her eyes at Phalen's nonchalant answer. "Don't worry," she said in a soothing tone. "I'm not pregnant." Molly waved the waiter on to get them their drinks.

This comment shorted out Mandy's already taxed brain. She stared at her sister's admission. "But, you said..." Mandy gaped at her sister. She leaned back as the waiter brought out their drinks.

"I said I *might* be pregnant," Molly said, a smile slipped across her face as she picked up her wine glass and hid behind it. "I never said I was."

Mandy stared at her, unable to process this. Her sister had told an untruth.

Molly set the glass back on the table.

Anger ran up Mandy's spine. "You *lied* to me!"

"No," Molly said as she held her finger up between them. "I didn't lie. There is always the possibility that I could be pregnant." She turned a smug smile toward Phalen. "Isn't that right, Phalen."

"Although birth control pills and condoms are affective most of the time, the only form of contraception that is one hundred percent guaranteed is abstinence," Phalen explained. "And since we haven't abstained, there's always the possibility that she *could* be pregnant." Phalen looked at Mandy. "But so could you." He leaned back in his chair,